PRAISE FOR
CHURCH OF SKATAN

"*Church of Skatan* is every bit the fun, counter-culture, kick-flip-a-demon-in-the-face sort of a story that you'd expect from the cover. But the real magic of *Skatan* comes from the Daughters of Eve, and Casey's creation of an enigmatic cult leader whose disciples will hunt you down and stick with you long after the back cover closes."

-William Sterling, author of *Dead Men's Chests*

"Satirical, clever and one hell of a wild ride. Damien Casey's *Church of Skatan* captivates with twists and turns that will have you asking how everything got so gnarly so quickly. He crafts a crew of characters that jump off the page threatening to drag you into this battle of cults."

-Alyson Hasson, author of *Island of the Unclaimed*

"Casey's style is beyond labels, and in *Church of Skatan*, he reaches new heights. A love letter to skating, a scathing critique of Evangelical Christianity, and a manic, blood-soaked story of trying to find acceptance."

-Elford Alley, author of *High Strangeness*

"Like Danzig jamming with the B52's to create a soundtrack for the best grindhouse movie of all time.

"Like your last ever summer vacation with childhood friends before you drift apart.

"Like totally radical, dude.

"Make no mistake this is Casey's strongest work to date."

-Adam Hulse, author of Below Economic Threshold

CHURCH OF SKATAN

DAMIEN CASEY

MADAXEMEDIA.COM

CHURCH OF SKATAN

DAMIEN CASEY

Mad Axe Media

Published by Mad Axe Media

madaxemedia.com

Edited by Candace Nola

Cover Art & Design by Joey Powell

Print ISBN: 979-8-9906858-4-0

E-Book ISBN: 979-8-9906858-5-7

This book is for George Romero.

Thank you for creating *Night of the Living Dead* and sparking my love for all things horror.

PROLOGUE

Who waters the plants in the Garden of Eden?

When God pulled the rib through the flesh of his first man like it was a branch stuck in mud, he expected someone to tend to the garden for eternity.

The woman wasn't interested.

The woman wasn't interested in the rules.

Why were they there?

What's the point of God giving us free will if we have to violate it to serve him?

The words always made Adam cringe when she asked.

He didn't want to piss off the voice in the clouds. The last time he did that, a great beast emerged from the lake; it had massive golden wings that were connected to a mouth filled with teeth. Its body was made up of a small army of writhing tentacles folding over one another. The smell was unlike anything else he had experienced. It smelled like violence, purity, blasphemy, and something called sex, all wrapped into one tight and cohesive package.

It had no eyes or conscience; it was a tool sent to make Adam cooperate. It was physical, emotional, and mental agony presented as a living and breathing being.

It hovered over a great elephant as if toying with its prey. The writhing mass of tentacles wrapped around the animal, severing its legs. It screamed out in pain. The mouth picked it apart little by little using only two of the teeth.

It was a display of the power and misery that could be bestowed upon Adam.

Adam told Eve of the victim. He showed her the small pile of body parts and hunks of flesh that continued to live on in eternal anguish.

Eve pointed at it, pointed at the sky, pointed at the apple tree, then shrugged.

Adam kept a close watch on her from that point.

He overheard God speaking with his once favorite, now exiled Angel, Lucifer, about the state of the Garden. Lucifer disagreed with the abominations walking in it that God had created. He told God they were disobedient bags of meat and juice that could pop just as easily as one of those apples thrown off a cliff.

God disagreed.

Lucifer turned into a snake and challenged the thought.

He showed Eve how hypocritical God's wisdom was.

How can he love you unconditionally when he has placed such a silly condition upon your existence?

How did he throw away the perfect companion, me, for... this?

The snake wrapped around the branches, locked its teeth into an apple, and grinned at Eve.

"Challenge your creator," the snake said. "Challenge his all-knowing, all-powerful ways. See how much of a child he is. You are nothing more than toys that he will cast away just as quickly as he cast me away."

Eve's mood grew dark. She snatched one of the apples from the tree and bit into it in defiance.

The jealousy of God became a cold and dry pillow, smothering all of the garden. Animals ran, great beasts buried their masses into the soil, the creatures of the oceans fled to the depths.

All around, animals began devouring one another.

Eve watched as two dogs began to fight. The snarls and attacks from each were filled with a hatred unlike anything she had ever seen. One of the dogs grabbed the other by its throat and forced it onto the ground. Blood flew from the victim's wound and cries fled from its lips. The two animals' children watched as their mother and father ripped each other to pieces.

"Away from me," said God as he flung both Adam and Eve from the garden.

Adam began to be different; he couldn't remove his eyes from Eve's nakedness. He became enraged that no part of her nakedness resembled the snake that caused this like his did.

One night, he found that her nakedness was the best place to hide this snake from the world, and it came with great pleasure.

Pleasure for Adam, pain for Eve; as often the story goes.

Two children were born from these moments of weakness from Adam.

Two children, who Eve looked upon with anger. These weren't her children. These were choices forced upon her in the same way the apple was.

Her children lay awake at night, watching as she sliced the skin of Adam's torso. They watched as she peeled back his eyelids to place wasps inside before sewing them shut. They watched as their father writhed in pain from the stings and lacerations; his body nothing more than gore and pain.

When he took his last breath, Eve came for the children.

The children were left in a mud puddle outside of a shack made of hay.

The man inside took them in and raised them as his own. He would later write the story of the first man and woman in a different way. He would then have to write the story of his two adopted sons. The story he manipulated.

Cain had become bitter, bitter about the snake that was constantly tangled around his ankle, telling him his mother was correct. His mother had every right to leave them for dead.

The snake kept a physical grip on his leg and an emotional one on his heart. He couldn't shake it. He couldn't look at Abel and not see how he and his brother were born from two miserable nights that led to their mother killing their father.

The snake was right.

It was late one night when Eve returned to finish the job. The snake riding on her shoulder like an omen of death. It slithered around her neck and head, whispering in her ear. It told her to end it all. To kill all of humanity here and now. End God's selfish little vanity project.

Eve shook her head and said no.

What could make these people more miserable than having to live?

She knew she could end their suffering or allow them to continue living in the knowledge of their irrelevance.

God didn't care about their suffering.

They all raped one another daily in a physical and otherworldly sense.

Let them live with the pain of knowing one side of the universe hates them, and the other is indifferent to their misery.

She decided to let them live.

The snake laughed and thought this was even better. Allow them to bring their own misery and death on one another in the same way God brought those things to him, and Adam brought those things to Eve.

They could hear Abel's muffled screaming as his brother shoved fire ants into his mouth. They could hear Cain ripping the flesh and muscle away from Abel's body and filling his insides with burning hot stones. They turned around and looked back just in time to see Cain bite out Abel's throat with his own teeth.

The old man approached Eve with tears in his eyes. "What in God's name have you done?" he said.

"There was no God for me," Eve said as she walked away.

The world went on.

Humanity killed each other over any small thing they could decide.

Wars were fought over different gods, wealth, and a black substance from below Earth's soil.

Wars were fought in backyards over one man coveting another's wife.

And as this story goes, wars were fought in abandoned churches that had indoor swimming pools.

In a dilapidated church in southern Ohio, two nineteen-year-old boys stand in the basement and stare at a swimming pool filled with brown and green water.

"I told you," says one. "My dad wouldn't make this shit up."

"Yeah, right," says the other. "Your dad told us that if we went out Old Lima Road far enough, we'd find a mini ramp and street section."

"I still believe him. He said that BMX guy built it at his house. Then he overdosed, and they tore it down."

"Sure, that's why there were fully grown trees all around the house."

"He did say it may be in the woods or in a building or something."

The boys look at the water. It's filled with dead leaves and floating branches. A film floats on top of the water, most likely from the rain leaking into the building and dripping into the pool for the past ten years.

Ethan Songen and Dylan Gillbourne sigh back and forth, hoping the other will come up with a solution.

"Maybe the drain is clogged?" says Dylan.

"Probably," says Ethan. "But I'm not taking a dive to find out."

"Maybe we could borrow your dad's sub pump?"

"Mom won't let me mess with any of his shit."

"He's been gone for two years."

"Yeah? I didn't know. I haven't been counting every day since junior year or anything."

"Sorry."

"It's cool. Anyway, we should call Billy and see if she wants to come down and check it out."

"Dude, she's not coming back for break. You know this."

"Last time I talked to her, she wasn't sure. She said she didn't know what Mandy was doing."

Dylan rolls his eyes.

Ethan shakes his head.

"Man, I'm sorry," says Dylan. "She fucking bailed on us. This Mandy chick takes her all across the state for shows. She's not coming back if she's staying on campus. And the only reason she will is because she isn't. We're second best here, man."

"Yeah," says Ethan. "I don't know. We're all best friends. You've got Maria at school; I don't get mad about that."

"That's because I still fucking call you, pecker-cheese. Besides, Maria was always going back home. Michigan is fucking far away."

"Yeah…"

Dylan holds his lips together with all of his might. He desperately wants to tell Ethan that if he had gone to college WITH Billy like they had both planned until last year, he wouldn't feel this way. Instead, he bites his tongue like he always does and stares into the muck of the pool.

"Real fucking mess, ain't it?" Dylan asks.

"Yeah," says Ethan. "Let's go see if Mom will let us use the sub pump."

They both take one last look at the water and leave.

They don't notice the bubbles rising to the surface from the bottom of the pool.

They don't hear the wind blowing around the bones in the rafters above the pool.

They don't see as the three bones from an infant's left hand fall off the ledge above and splash into the water below.

Somewhere, deep in the ground, something stirs. Something yearns for these visitors to return and drain one gate of its imprisonment.

SUMMER
2004

CHAPTER ONE

The alarm clock was going off again. This would be the last time for at least two months that Wilma Vallely had to hear that awful sound. She reached over and pushed the little button to shut it off. She rolled back to her back and stretched all of her limbs as far as they could go.

She used to have a routine; wake up, eat something for breakfast while watching either "Label Kills" or Consolidated's "Is What It Is". But her dorm room didn't come with a TV and her parents didn't want her to take the one from her room. She was lucky enough that her original roommate dropped out after the first semester, but less lucky when she found out the TV was hers and it would be leaving too.

After her morning breakfast, she used to go outside and skate in her driveway a little to stretch her legs. She didn't have anything but the flat concrete, and that was all she needed. She would do no complies, street plants, and other weird shit she learned from watching Public Domain.

Ethan and Dylan never understood how she could spend an hour having fun on the flat pavement without even a curb or anything. She never understood how they always had to skate like they were in some sort of imaginary school.

Get good.

Get on a flow team.

Go amateur.

Win Tampa Am.

Go pro.

Get shoe deal.

That was Ethan and Dylan's plan.

Her plan was simple: have fun.

Which she always did.

It was different since coming to school. The small college she attended didn't have any spots other than a small ledge and hubba running down a set of four stairs. The ledges were only about curb height, but she had a blast skating them after everything was shut down.

She didn't need to get kicked out of college just as quickly and easily as she had been kicked out of every skate spot back home. She decided to play it safe and wait until everyone was either back in their dorm or completely off campus before skating there. All it would take is campus security being called once, and she wouldn't even be able to cruise around from class to class.

She picked up the phone and dialed Ethan's number. She was supposed to let him know last night if she was coming home or not, but Mandy didn't give her an answer. Mandy was so flighty sometimes it was hard to tell if she didn't know or had known and already forgot.

"Hi, Wilma," Ethan's mom, Melissa, says as she answers.

"Hey, Melissa," says Wilma. "It's actually Billy, remember?"

"Sure, sure. I'm sorry. Hard to break the habit I've had for seventeen years. What's up?"

"Nothing really. I was supposed to call Ethan last night and let him know if I was coming home and I didn't get to because I never found out. I guess I should have called him to let him know that little bit, at least."

"He's okay. I think he's worried you two are drifting apart or something. You know how he gets now. He'll get over it. He did it with Dylan all year, too. Dylan just came home from school earlier. He'll be fine either way."

"I hope so. Is he around?"

"No, he went with Dylan to some abandoned church. Dylan's dad said there was an indoor pool or something. Bruce will lie to you kids about anything just to see if you believe it."

"You're totally right. Ok, well, I'm going to head over to Mandy's and see if she has any idea what she's doing, and then I'll call Ethan back later."

They say their farewells and Billy heads out. She grabs her deck on the way. She can cruise across campus one more time.

She heads outside and casually rolls down the sidewalk. She feels every crack under her wheels and has to pop over a few. She takes in the trees and foliage around her. She breathes in the summer air. Usually, she hates the summer. The air always feels like taking a drink of hot water. She passes her little spot and gives it a nod of her head. It's as if there is a mutual understanding here that she'll either see it tonight, or after summer. Either way, she feels the spot has its own personality and soul.

She rolls off a curb and has to Ollie back onto the sidewalk on the other side. She gains speed as she hits a slight hill and pops off curbs, then Ollies back onto them as fast as she can.

She whispers mean things about a guy she passes in a Real shirt wearing Nike skate shoes. She's a firm believer in the "Don't Do It" campaign. Skateboarding is an art form, not an Olympic sport. All of these corporations like Nike moving in make her sick. She skates for the love of skating; she believes in the culture. She thinks skateboarding should be kept as far away from the mainstream as possible.

2004 was shaping up to be the year that she was afraid everyone would skate with the intention of going pro.

If everyone skates, that's awesome, more people to skate with. But the second that turns into another money-making scheme in capitalist America, she's out.

Nike doesn't care about the culture or the art form. Nike doesn't care about skateboarding. Nike cares about dollars and how much they can make selling shoes in CCS.

She pops her deck up to her and walks up to Mandy's place. She sees Mandy's parents are already here. That must mean she's leaving.

She walks up to Mandy's dorm and is hugged by a blonde woman wearing a blue polo shirt.

"You have to be Billy, right?" the woman says. "I'm Catherine, Mandy's mom. That's Ed, and that little turd over there is Ryan."

Billy waves at them all and exchanges "nice to meet yous."

Mandy pecks her on the cheek and explains she wasn't sure if she was going home or not until they showed up today because Ryan was supposed to call and explain what was going on with the family vacation for a week straight, but being the little shit he is; he did not.

Billy says it's no problem. She'll just have her parents come get her and head home for the semester. She's only a couple hours away, so it isn't a huge deal. Besides, her parents were coming up this way anyway today to go to the mall, so it all works out.

She hangs with her girlfriend's family for a bit before they have to leave. They're heading on a cross-country road trip to the Grand Canyon because apparently Mandy is a part of the most wholesome family unit to ever exist.

Billy thinks that's cute.

When the farewells are done, she heads back across campus. She calls her parents and explains what is going on. Her dad seemed pissed. Nothing new there, honestly.

She calls Ethan again, this time he's home.

She tells him what's going on and he gets as excited as a squirrel who just found out it can grow nuts out of its toes. He rushes through, explaining that Dylan's dad wasn't lying; there is a pool. Totally skateable too.

She tells him she'll be there tomorrow, because she'll get home late tonight, and they can drain it.

She goes outside to mess around on the pavement for a little bit. She lands with her front foot too far back on a pop shove it and her board sails out from under her.

It hits a man in his shin. He just stands there staring at Billy.

He's dressed in heavy winter clothes, but it's mid-May, so what the fuck?

"Sorry," she says. "Got a little wonky on the landing."

The man doesn't respond.

She picks up her skateboard and walks a little further away from him.

He walks toward her, and she stops what she's doing.

"Hey," she says. "You fucking creep. What are you trying to pull? Trust me when I say I am not someone you want to kidnap. I can be really chatty and fucking annoying. So, leave me alone."

The man just stands.

"Not much of a talker, huh? Cool. Great. Awesome. Well, I'm going to go inside and lock the door because you're freaking me the fuck out."

The man opens his mouth, and she can see worms, ants, flies, and bumble bees swirling inside like he's trapped them all.

"Prepare for salvation," he says before closing his mouth and walking away. The bugs' bodies crunching sounds like bubble wrap being run over by a steamroller.

"Yeah!" she yells. "You can prepare for a tetanus shot because you've got an entire fucking insect exhibit in your mouth."

A fly buzzes past her ear and she jumps.

"Oh fuck!" she says as she swats and dances around.

When she gets into her room, she locks the door. She walks over to her desk and puts her head in her hands. She looks up and sees her reflection staring back at her. She covers the mirror with a towel and says, "I didn't say anyone's name five times. I didn't ask for all this weirdness."

She looks out her window to see if the guy is still walking somewhere and can't find him.

Come on, Mom and Dad, she thinks.

CHAPTER
TWO

She was born in a hospital in a city she never knew the name of. She stumbled out of her fifth foster home at fifteen and never looked back. She made a life out of the desires of old men and the wallets of the rich for the next ten years.

On her sixteenth birthday, she was in a bedroom where she heard a man talking to his wife in the other room after she came home early. She spent her seventeenth birthday on the seventh floor of a New York skyscraper under a desk. She spent her eighteenth birthday watching one brother try to kill the other while the one who purchased an hour of her time kept saying, "She just turned legal today." On her nineteenth birthday, she started hearing the voice of Eve.

Cecily was never sure if that was really her first name, or if her last name was Simpkins, Joel, McKeller, Ratliff, or Gibbs. The first name stayed the same, but the last name changed time and time again. When she was on her own, she decided she didn't want a last name. A last name tied her to something other than jobs and Eve.

Eve told her where to find the right men. Eve told her how to hold their sack just right and where to place the pocketknife to get them to give her all their money. Eve showed her how to activate the small video camera she stole from a pawnshop for blackmail.

Without Eve, she wouldn't be getting a steady payout of forty-three grand a week from the men she had videos of. Men who thought sending a thousand bucks to a woman they hadn't seen in over fifteen years was better than whatever their wives would charge them for alimony.

At the age of forty-two, Cecily had built up a small empire and a small group of followers known as The Daughters of Eve. She showed them the ways Eve showed her. She introduced them to her tech wizard, who set up all the payments.

Only one of forty-three men had ever threatened to stop paying. He paid up real fast when a woman called his wife's phone and said she wanted to talk.

Too close to home for him, apparently.

She could feel them working behind the scenes against her, though. She had heard chatter that one of the men had terminal cancer and was going to spill it all. The others begged him not to do it, but apparently, he found God.

Fucking death bed Christians ruining a good thing. How exactly does someone find God? That's what she always wanted to know. Was the guy just looking for his lost remote and then, VOILA! THERE'S

GOD! Was he just sort of hiding in some bushes and got discovered by a gardener? Was it a cosmic game of Where's fucking Waldo?

She had already planned to sever ties at the start of the year, but this just hurried the process. She instructed her tech man to take one huge ten grand lump sum from each account and send an email to each that said their loan was now paid off. Ten grand to these men wouldn't be but a dime in the ocean. She paid her guy twenty grand to erase all of her trails, erasing her completely from existence so no one could ever track Cecily or one of the fifty names she had used.

When that was completed, her seven disciples held the man down. They put a gun in his hand and forced him to pull the trigger when the barrel was touching the roof of his mouth. Another loose end tied up. Another man's brain that had too much knowledge splattered against a wall.

Together, the eight women travelled across the country in an illegal RV. If they were pulled over, they paid the cop off and went about their way. There's no one more underpaid or corrupt than the police force in America and Cecily would proudly sport a "blue lives matter" sticker on the back of the RV for all the favors their greed had done her.

She did kill one every now and again. She fucking hated cops.

She hated any man who claimed authority over her.

It was her life and had been since she was a teen. She had the scars, both physical and emotional, to prove it.

Her seven disciples all had similar scars.

Rhonda from her abusive father when she was twelve. She asked if they could watch a different TV show because the news was oh so boring. He beat her with a steel toe'd boot until her mother stepped in. Cecily met her in a bar. Rhonda was beating a man with a wine bottle because he said he was going to shove his size thirteen steel toe work boot up her ass.

Mary from a dog that attacked her at eight when she tried to take its food so she could eat. She hadn't eaten in a week. The old man who owned the store that had its backdoor in the alleyway she slept fed a dog every night before he left. She couldn't take seeing the thing eat while she starved one more time. She tried to take the porkchop and found her face locked in the dog's jaws. Cecily met her when she was working at a dog pound. Mary would beat dog owners that abandoned their dogs because "they didn't have time for them" and feed them to the strays in town.

Beth from an aunt when she had her finger snapped backwards for stealing at nine. She had asked for the money to go to the theater because her mother and father said no. It was just five bucks. When her aunt said no, she decided it was time to take life into her own hands. Her aunt caught her and snapped her finger backwards while lecturing her about what The Bible has to say on thieves. Cecily met her at a video store. Beth would let kids rent whatever they wanted for free. If parents said no, she would follow them home. She would sneak into their houses while they were asleep and break their fingers.

Eliza from a professor's wife who shoved her down a flight of stairs at twenty. Eliza had known Professor Camington was having an affair. He told her he was separated from his wife. His wife knew about everything he reassured her. Turned out that was false when she kissed him in front of his wife and felt all thirty stairs hitting her as she fell. Cecily met her at a singles bar. Eliza would pick up men who lied about being single and tie them up outside of the house on their driver's license.

Brittany from a racist guy in Tennessee who said people like her weren't allowed in his bar at nineteen. When Brittany asks if it was because she was black or because she had a brain cell, the man says, "Both." He beat her close to death with a chunk of wood he kept behind the bar. Cecily met her one night in a park. Their meeting was tender and not based on violence. That is, until a man walked by and called them dyke bitches. That was when Brittany showed how cruel she could be as she pinned the man down and pulled his tongue out of his mouth. She held it there and slowly put weight on his head to close his jaws, forcing him to bite off his own tongue. Brittany became Cecily's favorite pupil that night.

Deanna from the pastor of her church when he found out she was masturbating at seventeen. She was in her room; she had thought her parents had left when her mother came barging in her room asking about the car keys. Her mother screamed and ran away. Two hours later, the pastor was there giving her an exorcism to evict a sex-demon from her body. The exorcism consisted of slashes to her pubic area with a small razor while the man read bible verses. Cecily met her at a strip club. She would wait around enjoying the show until a man who claimed to be a Christian came in. She would then invite him to her place and drug him. When he was asleep, she would slice the bottoms of his feet with a razor and leave him stranded miles away from civilization. Naked too.

Gail the neighbor boy who held her down and poured boiling hot soapy water in her mouth for cussing at four. Gail had told the boy he was a real son of a bitch for hitting her with a stick. The boy said his mom washed his mouth out with soap when he cussed. Gail said it sounded fair. She just didn't expect the boy to boil the water, but she assumed he knew what he was doing. Cecily met her at a therapy session. She would follow a man that looked even remotely like that young boy and cut out their tongues in an alleyway.

All eight of them had heard the voice in their moments. All eight had been led to one another. All eight had washed their hair in the blood of holy men all across the nation.

Every town has a church, and every town has a man of God who needs to meet an end.

A man in Wyoming begged Deanna not to slice the skin between his fingers and leave him in the baptismal tub to bleed out.

A man in Idaho had said all of them would burn in hell if they forced him to drink that glass of bleach.

Cecily's favorite so far was the guy who tried to use the Bible as a shield. She brushed it away and pushed his frail, seventy-six-year-old frame to the ground. From there, she placed the front of the book on the tip of his nose. The other women held him down while she slowly put all of her weight onto her left foot and sent the cartilage of his nose into his brain.

The Daughters of Eve had pulled into a small town in Michigan when they saw the sign in the rest area. A map behind the glass showed the state of Ohio. The paint had faded. A snake was drawn, its body making a circle around a small town in southern Ohio.

This would be the place.

This would be where The Right Hand of Adam and the other men of God would have imprisoned the last angel.

Brittany smashed the glass with a large rock she found outside, then unpinned the map, rolled it, and handed it to their driver, Beth.

Outside, Cecily set a wristwatch on the ground and smashed it. She cut her finger and let the blood trickle over the broken machinery. The wires, gears, and metal formed a small humanoid shape with the clockface as the head.

"Clockwise for yes," Eve instructed. "Counter for no. Did you bring us here to see the snake?"

Clockwise.

"Is the snake where we need to go?"

Clockwise.

"Is this the end of things?"

Counter-clockwise.

The watch-person sat down and fell apart, becoming a pile of machinery.

Cecily brushed the pieces into the grass with her foot.

"Looks to me like it's time to collect the feathers of an angel," Cecily said as the RV pulled out of the parking lot, leaving behind a traveling preacher who was burning alive, tied up, in his car.

They were miles away when the fire finally reached the gas tank.

CHAPTER THREE

When Andrew left his wife and kid, he wasn't worried about all the shit he had in the garage. The only thing on his mind was whatever freedom he needed to obtain. That freedom apparently meant you couldn't be tied down by things like a table sander or a sub pump.

Ethan and his mom went back and forth for twenty minutes about going into the garage. She refused to look at the stuff. It was like she thought looking at Andrew's abandoned items would make her relive the trauma of giving all of his clothes to Goodwill. She couldn't face that ghost again, and she had no plans to.

To her, it seemed to Ethan, even letting him go into the garage was an admittance of the ghost that haunted their lives without even opening cabinet doors. Ethan thought it would be kind of badass if his dad was a ghost. At least then maybe he could do that wild thing from the movie *Ghost Dad* where the dad comes through the phone. His dad wasn't that kind of ghost. His dad had become the kind of ghost that just vanishes without even a note saying he would be back.

Facebook and other social media searches found nothing. Wherever Andrew had gone, he didn't plan on being found.

Could his dad be a cooler kind of ghost? Yes.

But, no, all Ethan gets is a bunch of abandoned tools that his mom won't even admit are there. She won't even park her car in the garage anymore. The neighbors are probably starting to talk about that. The whole room just sits there untouched, like it's a blemish on the face of the Earth. It's a quarantine area that no one is allowed to enter.

Ethan had thought of hanging a sign that says, "No admittance! Dad who bailed stuff inside!"

"You know what, Ethan," Torrie says. "If some little pool to skate-board in is more important to you than your father, go ahead. Take the sub pump. Take all the stuff."

He wasn't sure what exactly his dad had left for. So, he couldn't exactly pinpoint exactly what his dad had decided was more important than Ethan and Torrie. In that case, yeah, the pool was more important than his father. The pool was there. The pool would provide hours of skating for him and his friends. The pool would provide a private hangout where the three of them could get away from the nonsense of being at home.

He walks into the garage and looks around; everything is covered in a thin layer of sawdust. His father built birdhouses all the time for the neighbors. So many that it's gotten near impossible for Ethan and Torrie to leave home without some reminder in the form of a wooden bird feeding station. Every time they go to the store, they have to be reminded of Andrew's passion. *Really,* Ethan thinks, *that should have been the first sign of trouble; who spends that much time building birdhouses?*

"Birds don't even live in stupid fucking houses, Dad," Ethan says to himself. "They live in nests."

He spits on the birdhouse his father was working on before he left. Spits on the memories of his father. Spits on the time his father wouldn't come see how Ethan had just started consistently landing a kickflip because some stupid old woman needed a birdhouse.

Maybe that's why he left? He couldn't take having to build any more birdhouses for the stupid fucking neighbors, so he bounced.

Sorry, Mrs. White, you're a lovely lady, but I cannot build one more birdhouse. I can't do it. I'll fucking snap. It'll be a massacre. That blood will be on your hands.

Ethan found the sub pump and pushed it outside. He'd wait until tomorrow to ask his mom to drive him and Dylan to the church again. If Billy was home and ready to go drain the thing, they wouldn't even have to ask Torrie. Which at this point may be better?

He looked at the small pump and realized it was going to take forever to drain a full pool with. Maybe the drain really was clogged? Maybe all they had to do was figure that out?

When he went back into the house, he heard his mom crying in the living room. He walked in and sat beside her.

"Mom," he said. "You know he isn't coming back, right?"

"Yeah," Torrie says, wiping the tears from her eyes. "I just wish... You don't deserve this."

"Mom, I'm an adult. I thought the guy was lame since I was thirteen. With all those lame fucking birdhouses. Come on, you're an adult. Get a better hobby."

"Yeah," a smile cracks Torrie's face lightly. "He did love those things."

"More than us! I have an idea..."

Ethan jumps up and goes back to the garage. He grabs the birdhouse he spat on and takes it to the backyard. One useful thing Andrew did was build a nice little fire pit. He sits the birdhouse in the center and goes back inside for lighter fluid, matches, and his mom.

He drags her out by her hand and lights the birdhouse on fire.

His mom takes a long sip from the bottle of Merlot she's been carrying around all evening. "You know," she says. "When I met your father, he had big plans. He was going to start his own business. Building those."

She points the bottle at the burning house.

"He said, 'Torrie, I'm going to build us a house with all the money I make from these houses.' He said we were going to be birds and shit. How fucking stupid is that? I don't want to be a bird, Ethan. I'm a goddamn fucking human being and I deserve to be treated as one."

She stands up and throws the wine bottle at the house. It misses and flies out into the backyard.

Ethan and Torrie both slowly start laughing about that. Even in anger, nothing can seem to go right. Can't even have some big dramatic display without missing the target.

She hugs her son and says, "I love you, Ethan. We're going to get back on track. We don't need him. Go to school next year. You've taken enough time off in life."

Ethan hugs his mom tight and says, "I love you, Mom. Even if you did marry a birdhouse-loving asshole loser."

They stand together and watch the birdhouse fold into itself from the flames.

CHAPTER FOUR

Dinner was Hamburger Helper with a side of shells and cheese. Dylan was lost. Weren't those the same thing? Noodles and cheese are the same thing as noodles and cheese.

He didn't want to say it out loud because at least his father had tried. He wasn't much of a cook, usually when it was his dinner night the family ended up with takeout. The last time he cooked, it was chicken tenders cooked in the microwave. That night they all had stomachaches, and the bathroom was the most exclusive club in the country.

"Dad," says Dylan's little brother, Reese, "why did you make noodles and cheese with hamburger, and a side of noodles with cheese?"

Their mom, Lauren, started to laugh under her breath.

"Okay, okay," says Bruce. "Y'all think you can do better?"

"I don't know," says Lauren. "I kind of like how the two types of cheese taste a little different."

Bruce shook his head and put a little of each on his fork. "I don't know what I'm doing," he says with a shrug.

They eat in that awkward silence of trying not to laugh. The awkward thing where you know if you make eye contact with someone, you'll lose it. Every now and then, one of them lets slip a little giggle that they cover up with a cough or a sniff of their nose.

Lauren eventually slips and starts laughing.

Dylan notices both meals even have shell-shaped macaroni, and he loses it.

Bruce just shakes his head and keeps eating while he's laughing.

"What's for dessert?" Dylan asks. "Cake flavored cake?"

They all laugh, but Bruce gets up and leaves. He comes back with a cake mix that says, "Birthday cake flavored cupcakes."

"Great," Bruce says. "Now my son's a psychic. Did y'all find that pool, anyway?"

"Yeah, it's just filled with water."

"They probably left it half full when they left. That church was weird. I went there when I was... Lauren, how old were we when we hung out with Harriet?"

"Eh, fifteen-ish?" Lauren says.

"Probably so. Anyway, we went there, and they were all about making sure they blessed the water in the pool. Who cares? People piss in swimming pools. Do you think their piss is blessed then?"

"I don't know," says Dylan. He's used to his father's rants about how he thinks some things are a bit... stupid.

"I can tell you how to drain it," Bruce says.

"How?"

"So, you go down behind the church, out behind that basement. There's a hill, yeah? It has a big sewage drain system that flows down into the river. The place was built before septic tanks. Anyway, if you go down that hill, you'll see a little lid you can open to see the channel. Is that what they call it? I dunno. It's a big concrete tube, essentially. Probably three feet around. There's a drain in that pool that drops all the water down into that. Probably just have to pull the plug. The filtration system was set up quite a bit differently if I remember right. Not that you goons care about filtration."

They finished eating both varieties of cheesy noodle with mostly small talk. The usual this and that of the day. Reese was on break from school. He would be a sophomore next year. Dylan felt bad for him. High school was rough for Dylan. He was always known to his classmates as sort of the funny one. He didn't know why. Sure, he liked to joke around a bit, but that didn't mean *everything* he said was some sort of a joke.

That's how his peers had always seen him though. Nothing serious was ever said if Dylan was saying it. Even serious conversations were taken as Dylan having a laugh. He was beginning to feel like he just wasn't being taken very seriously at all.

College was different. He met Maria there. Maria made him feel like he could be a complex person in another's eyes. Not just some weird carnival act that was always talking in jokes. Maria let him have his moments of sadness and embraced him. She let him have his anger and soothed him. Most importantly, she sat with him in his loneliness.

It was their fourth date when Dylan admitted that he felt alone. He had close friends, sure, but not THAT one friend or significant other.

Even his brother had a friend that he could talk to about everything. It was even harder seeing Ethan and Billy being that close. He was close to both of them, sure, they were his best friends. But he didn't have that bond with either of them that they had with each other.

That's why this particular summer has been such a pain in the ass. Billy and Ethan were like long-lost siblings. But this past year, they didn't spend as much time together. Dylan knows that's what happens with real siblings, that's what happens when people start dating, that's especially what happens when one person goes away for a year while the other freezes their life to spend another year at home grieving a man who abandoned them. Ethan was never going to see what he did to hurt Billy, and Billy was never going to see what she did to hurt Ethan.

Should Billy have stayed home?

Should Ethan have abandoned his mom?

Neither question has an answer, and friendship isn't that clear cut.

Dylan was just hoping Billy would actually show up tomorrow and things could go back to normal for a few months. He didn't need the constant conversations with Ethan about how much he missed Billy. They always made him feel second best. He just wanted to pretend his friends were being normal again and get on with life. Maybe they could talk it out over the summer. They've had fights before and didn't go all "Look Back and Laugh" by Minor Threat just yet, so why can't they this time?

Dylan knew Ethan felt replaced by Mandy. He thought Billy could only focus on one or the other. That's just not true. Dylan has managed to focus on his friends and Maria for the past year. Why can't they both see that and focus on him and what he needs a little?

Because he's the eternal funny man.

He's the eternal cheer up man.

He's the one who tells the joke or does something to make everyone laugh. He never feels loneliness or sadness.

He was getting himself a bit down about it all. About his place in the universe.

This is what Maria was good at. She talked him through his issues, made him feel less lonely, she became that person he could lean on. He needed that. She needed that. It was the first mutual understanding he had ever had.

Recently, a new wave of anxiety had started attacking Dylan, one where Maria would forget about him over summer break. She'd go home and forget he existed. When he explained this to her, she reassured as she always does, but Dylan still felt a little off put.

Maria started taking notes in her planner, which she never left home without, about all the times in the day she thought about Dylan. It was a sweet gesture that made him love her even more.

He's had people like this before, but it always ends the same. They move on to something better.

He resists the urge to call her; instead, he goes out into the garage to skate the flat rail his dad welded together.

He throws in a CD, "Full Circle" by Pennywise. He grabs his deck and starts pushing around. He does a couple of flat Ollies to stretch his legs. He lands a couple heel flips.

The last time he tried to 50/50 the rail, his board went wonky, and he fell forward hitting his shins on the rail and his face on the ground. Every time he tries now, all he can picture is that incident. He Ollies and throws his board away from him before turning sideways with his legs on either side of the rail.

He's starting to get a little pissed off about how his brain is faking him out.

He hits a couple board slides to build his confidence. He pushes off hard before he can think; he snaps the tail of his board on the ground; he turns into position in the air. He feels his trucks lock on the railing. He balances it out for less than an inch. That's enough to show him it doesn't always have to end the same way.

He calls Ethan and tells him he doesn't think they'll need the sub pump.

CHAPTER
FIVE

The church sits at the end of a quarter-mile gravel road. It's the only building on the road and all the houses have been demolished. It's surrounded on all sides by trees. It almost sits in its own little cubby hole created by the surrounding woods. Behind the church is a hill that runs deeper into the woods.

The first time they got here, Ethan's mom dropped them off, and they walked. Dylan doesn't have a vehicle because he's been in school and can walk everywhere on campus. Ethan shares a car with his mom.

Today they had Billy.

They approached the church and took it in. Standing there on a slight hill surrounded by woods, it looked like something out of a movie. It looked like a church you would see in movies from the fifties, windows along the side, huge wooden doors, cross on top.

The only way to get in is through a side door that's been busted open. It opens to the stairs that lead down to the basement. The door at the top leading into the church remains locked. All they can explore is one single room, which looks like a classroom and the poolroom.

The pool is enclosed on all sides by the concrete of a basement. A couple of shower rooms are on one wall labeled boys and girls. Behind the deep end of the pool, the whole wall is made of glass. A sliding glass door sits in the middle to enter and exit. Outside of this door is a hillside, and an abandoned shed that they assume was used to store pool supplies but now just houses the broken-down filtration system.

"This is it, huh?" Billy says as she looks at the filled pool. She watched as a frog jumped into it when they arrived. That presents a whole new set of issues in her mind. Where are the frogs going to go when they make this their own personal skatepark?

"Yeah," says Dylan. "We just gotta find the drain. It's probably clogged. If we do that, it'll be good to go."

"You don't think we're going to have to clean out all the dead bugs, leaves, and random frog shit?"

"Well, I mean, yeah... we'll have to do that."

"Are you sure there's even transition there? What if it's just square walls, you know what I mean?"

Dylan and Ethan look at each other. Neither had considered the possibility that the walls would just be straight up and down at ninety-degree angles. They just assumed this was a dream come true. Dylan didn't even ask his dad about the sides.

"Hold on," says Ethan. He leaves the basement through the sliding glass door. The builders must have thought at least seeing the outside was going to be enough. Either way, he's thankful because the wall of windows provides enough light for them to see what they're doing.

He goes out and finds the biggest fallen tree limb he can find and comes back in. He puts it down in the water and slowly lowers it into the deep end of the pool along the wall. Sure enough, the stick moves toward the middle as it starts hitting the slight curve.

This thing is skateable.

Dylan pumps his fist in the air like he's just won the lottery.

"Thank god," says Ethan.

"Ok," says Billy. "Now, how do you both plan to find the drain? I'm not diving in."

"Jesus Christ, Billy," says Dylan. "You've been gone all summer. The first thing you do is run us into the ground about how stupid we are for thinking this would work. Why can't you offer a solution instead of making us feel like assholes?"

"If something seems too good to be true, it's probably too good to be true."

"Are you my dad now? That's what my dad says. Are you my fucking dad?"

"No, because if I were your dad, I wouldn't let you sleep under my roof knowing you use Grind King trucks with an American flag print."

"Dude, I told you the CCS guy put the wrong number. It was supposed to be the all black Ed Templeton. Not this weird ass American flag print Toy Machine deck."

"Yeah... sure... when you said you loved Bush, I didn't think you meant George Bush..."

"Oh, fuck off, Billy. You know I wasn't even old enough to vote. And I'm not voting for him next cycle."

"Your shit says otherwise. You go ahead and vote for him. Just let me know how it feels when you wake up in a desert wearing combat boots."

"FUCK!" yells Ethan. "Stop. We all know Dylan can't read for shit, so he definitely told the CCS dude the wrong number. We also know all about your political shit. Can we try to drain this fucking thing?"

Ethan pushes the limb out further in the deep end, looking for the drain. He's thinking that maybe he can loosen whatever is clogging it up. He pokes around for ten minutes.

Dylan walks off to look for something to use and comes back with a large black plastic trash bin.

"I have an idea," Dylan says as he sets the trash can in the water. "I can use it like a little boat and go out there with the stick for balance and find the drain."

"Dylan," Billy says. "I think that is the dumbest idea you've ever had. But also, the smartest."

"Yeah," says Ethan. "Not sure it will work, but I'm not opposed to watching you try."

They lay the bin on its side and Dylan crawls in. They slowly push it off the ledge and into the water, turning it into a weird makeshift boat. It seems to be balanced okay and Dylan shrugs. Ethan hands him the branch and he starts using it as an oar.

"Guys," Dylan says. "This is insane. What if there's a crocodile in here?"

"Don't be a dumbass," says Ethan.

"Those things can't survive in Ohio," says Billy.

"My dad said that this guy bought one, and it got loose in the river," says Dylan.

"But how would it have gotten here from the river?" asks Ethan.

"Crocodiles have legs, Ethan. They can walk, you know?"

Dylan pushes the stick around at the bottom of the pool. He hits something with the branch and says, "Shit, I think I got it." When he tries to pull the stick up, the bin topples to one side and messes up his balance.

He's rocking back and forth with waves splashing into the bin yelling, "Crocodile! Crocodile!" The bin tips over and sends Dylan into the murky water.

Ethan and Billy choke on their laughter. They realize they have to at least make sure Dylan isn't dead before they laugh.

Dylan's head emerges from the water covered in a weird film and dead leaves.

"Goddamnit," Ethan says. "I really thought that would work. This water is weirdly warm, though. It feels thick too."

"Thick?" asks Billy.

"Yeah, like oil or something. I don't know. Fucking gross. Help me out."

"Wait, wait, wait," says Ethan. "You're already in there, you already smell like shit. Try to go down there and find the drain."

"No fucking way. What about the crocodile?"

"There isn't a crocodile!" Ethan and Billy yell at the same time.

Dylan rolls his eyes. He moves his head back and forth. "You guys owe me big," he says before submerging himself.

He comes back up and gasps for air.

"It's fucking gross in here!" Dylan yells.

"No one asked you to be all Christopher Columbus," says Billy.

Dylan goes back under and this time, a giant bubble hits the surface before him. His head pops out, and he has the biggest smile.

"Got it!" he says as he swims toward the side of the pool. "There were a bunch of dead leaves in the grate. I just took the grate out."

They can already see the water level lowering.

"Nice," says Ethan. "Want to go change and skate in town for a bit? Then come back and see what cleaning we have to do?"

"Cleaning?" says Billy. "I thought we'd just let Dylan roll around like a mop."

Dylan splashes water up at them as he climbs out.

"Thank you for caring so much," he says as he grabs Billy in a hug.

"Fuck off!" she yells as she runs from him.

Ethan smiles and thinks about how it's just like it's always been.

They go out the sliding doors and walk over the hill. They can see the water flowing through an exposed pipe, just like Dylan's dad said it would. The water is a dark green, almost black. Billy squats down and puts her finger in it.

"He's right," she says. "It does feel like oil. It's water, but it's like oil thickness."

"Maybe it's from the dirt?" Ethan asks.

"Probably the crocodile shit."

The water drains through a network of pipes. It makes the shape of the crucifix over a hollowed-out room.

Inside the room, something stirs and tries the gateway.

Still locked in by one gate.

CHAPTER SIX

A nd the congregation says, "Amen!"

The sermon today really resonated with a lot of people. It really hit home. Talking hitting the nail on the head kind of stuff.

What do you do with a congregation that's heavily medicated by the anti-depressants of man and not the spirit of Jesus?

Tell them to get closer to their father and creator.

Tell them to reach out to him.

Tell them in their darkest times he is the lighthouse and your emotions are the blackened sea rolling over you. He will guide you. He will get you to shore.

As it says in Jeremiah 29:11, "For I know the plans I have for you, declares the Lord, plans for peace and not for evil, to give you a future and a hope."

God would never put anything on his children that he knew they couldn't handle. If a person goes through the worst suffering of their life, the good is so much more appreciated. When the scripture speaks of a rich man having as much of a chance of seeing Heaven as a camel passing through the eye of a needle; it means that people who are rich and without trial, they won't appreciate the splendor of God's glory.

Pastor Jay sits in his office feeling the afterglow of God's word made truth passing through him. He can't talk to the congregation after; too many of them all at once. They all want to praise him and tell him how wonderful he is. His ego has been getting the better of him and he's forgotten whether he was truly preaching God's word or Jay Barnett's words.

He walked in on his sixteen-year-old daughter, running a razor over her wrists three nights ago. He had a whole sermon planned around something completely different. He doesn't remember what that was at this point.

When he saw Lisa's arm bleeding all over an old t-shirt, she had laid down on her bedroom floor. Everything else left his mind. He grabbed her and forced her to pray with him. They read scripture. They listened to praise music.

Lisa said it didn't matter. Life was hopeless. She didn't feel God's love the same as her parents, and she didn't think she ever would. Already in her sixteen years, she had been beaten by an ex-boyfriend at a football game; other students filming instead of helping. She had been harassed by those students' friends when they got into trouble. Her parents refused to even consider relocating because the church was here. She just wanted to get an hour away. Just enough distance between her and Heath, her ex. She had to pass him every day in the hallway at school; sure, he would be graduating next year but that didn't change the fact that he followed her home every day.

Every time she parked her car, she heard the horn honk as he passed by in his truck. That sound filled her with dread and anxiety. Then there were the phone calls from the students' parents saying she had to do something to Heath. He wasn't the type of boy to hit a woman.

Well, newsflash, Heath was exactly that type of boy. His mother had a black eye two years ago to prove it. Lisa had a broken nose, busted lip, chipped tooth, and fractured right arm to prove it.

Pastor Jay knew that Heath's parents watched his every move. They were the highest tithe in the building. Most of his family's income came from them.

So, what if the kid made a mistake?

Didn't his wife, Carmen, make him angry when he was a kid?

Kids argue, that's what they do. Some kids just don't have the self-control to not lose their temper. This was more on Lisa for not getting away from Heath when his anger showed up the first time. Now she expects Jay to uproot the whole family?

For what?

To go back to working as a busboy at Texas Roadhouse while Carmen has to unbutton her shirt two buttons lower than she's comfortable with to get tips?

That's no way to live.

Lisa was just going to have to accept that students bully each other. She needed to learn to lean on God and get through this.

He calls Carmen and asks how Lisa is doing. Apparently not great, because Carmen couldn't get her to come to lunch after church. She just wanted to go home. She was pissed off that Jay used a whole sermon to lecture her.

Jay rubbed his temples and leaned back in the chair. It wasn't just for her. It was for all the people in the church who were suffering. Can't these people just say, "Yeah, this isn't the best, but God will make it right"? Of course not. They're all weak. That's why they need the love of God.

Someone knocks on his office door. He can't imagine who it would be other than his assistant, Steven. Sure enough, Steven pokes his head in and tells Jay there's someone in a lot of trouble that needs to speak with him. He stood up, straightened his collar, and walked to the door.

Standing beside Steven was a woman of around twenty-five. She had brown curly hair and green eyes. She was new to the church; Jay would have recognized someone this distinctly beautiful. He invited her into his office and they both sat in his "lounge" area he used for counseling. He sits in a leather chair and the woman sits across from him on a sofa.

"Can I get you something to drink, Miss..." Jay says.

"Eliza," the woman says. "I'm okay. I'm just really needing to pray with someone."

"What's the issue?"

"I've been depressed. Nothing makes sense. I feel hopeless. I feel as though I'm a person who was supposed to die in her mother's womb and left her soul there. I can't feel God anywhere I look."

"Yet here you are. You must have felt something."

"I have been walking for months. I left my abusive husband and just started walking. He isolated me from my friends and family. He made sure I had nowhere to go. I was passing through this town, following the river, when I saw your church. Your message was what I needed to hear. Can I show you something?"

"Of course."

Eliza pulls back the sleeve of her cardigan. There are fresh wounds all over her right arm. Jay thinks it looks like she got stuck in a lawnmower, but he knows this is the same devil that his daughter suffers from.

"Oh my," he says. "This is very close to home. I think you were supposed to be here. I don't think it's an accident you were guided here. Can we pray?"

Eliza's eyes turn to overflowing glasses of tears. She nods and Jay moves to the sofa and holds her hands in his.

"Father, dear Jesus. We are coming to you today because your daughter Eliza is suffering. The weight of the world is being thrust upon her and her back is giving out. Lord, we ask for just a little more strength. Give her the strength to overcome this. Give her the strength to love her life again, lord. Let her love the life that you have given her as she should."

"That's what you're asking for?"

Jay looks at Eliza. She's staring at him with her eyes wide open. There's a different person in those eyes than the one he met. This one isn't a wounded sheep; this one is a tiger stalking its prey. This woman isn't hurt, this woman has come to hurt.

"I..." he says. He can't find the right words to say.

"If God can do anything. Anything at all, right? Why can't he just... POOF! Make my depression go away?"

"That's not really how it works."

"That's how it works when YOU lose your car keys though, isn't it? You pray and VOILA! there they are! You need the store to still have a cake because you forgot it's your wife's birthday? CAKE YOU SHALL FUCKING HAVE!"

Eliza is standing up. She hovers over Jay; the power dynamic has shifted so quickly that Jay doesn't know what to say or do. He can't even think.

What about this?" she says. "What about the kids starving? What about babies born addicted to heroin? What about me? There was no God for me."

When she finishes, she stands silently. The room is filled with tension and Jay tries to diffuse it.

"I get you're upset. Sometimes things aren't fair. Let me get Steven in here and we can really talk this out. We can really figure it all out."

Eliza smirks and shouts, "STEVEN!"

The door creaks open and Steven stumbles in falling down. He's followed by seven other women.

"Great job, Eliza," says the one who walks over and embraces her. "I'm Cecily. We are the daughters of Eve. And you, you're fucked."

One of the women lifts Steven's head from the ground by his hair and slams his face back down. She rubs his face into the carpet like he's a dog with an abusive owner and he just shit all over the nicest pair of shoes in the house.

One of the other women walks to Jay's desk and throws his computer monitor on the floor.

The one named Cecily walks to the smashed electronics and whispers to the machinery.

From inside, the wires writhe like tentacles, each wrapping around a piece of shattered glass. Wires pull a mound of broken electronics from inside the screen like an octopus made of electronics. The creature moves toward Steven and all eight of its limbs slash at his face with glass. One piece of glass is stuck up his right nostril. It slices through all the way up to the eye socket. Jay can hear the glass scraping the skull of the man. When it reaches the eyeball, the glass pops it out like the center of an olive.

Steven cries out in agony and eventually passes out from the pain.

"What do you want?" Jay begs.

"How did I know that would be the next thing he said," says Cecily. "What do you think, Deanna? Should we let him off this easy?"

"The word of God shall punish like a whip," says Deanna.

"That's what her pastor told her," says Cecily. "She's still pretty bitter about it. Of course, I would be too if a seventy-year-old man beat me with a Bible and then whipped my pussy with a belt. How would you like it if someone did that to your balls? Yeah, I know, you're one of those new school guys. All New Testament and no Old. Give me that vengeful god. Give me the God that destroyed Sodom and Gomorrah for getting a little freaky with it. Give me the God that gave a man and his wife a son, then demanded they kill him to prove their love. That's what I want. I want to kill him. I don't want to kill sandals-wearing vegan Jesus. He's a pussy. He wouldn't even try to fight. What a fucking sham."

"Please," Jay says. "Just tell me what you want."

"Ugh. Ok. There's a church around here. It's been abandoned. Maybe by a lake or pond. There's something sealed underneath by two gates. One would be holy water mixed with anointing oil; hence, the pond or lake. The other is more of a metaphysical thing. The right words, the right symbol, a little blood from a virgin; gross, I know. But you know how these old curses are. Always has to be a virgin."

"I have no idea."

Cecily grabs a pen from his desk and stabs him in the hand.

"Shhhhhhh," she says. "I'm not quite done. Wait... I am. Sorry. An abandoned church. Let's start there."

"There's one just outside of town. It had an indoor swimming pool. Some youth engagement plan. It didn't work. The ex-pastor goes here now."

"Too cool! Now, how do I get there?"

"Couldn't you have just asked somebody? Isn't all of this unnecessary?"

Another woman walks over and punches him in the face. She has scars on her own face that look like the bite of a dog.

"Mary!" says Cecily. "I'm sorry. She doesn't like it when we watch movies, and the antagonist has to lay out exactly why they're doing what they're doing for the audience's pleasure. No, Mary, this may be a logical question. Why wouldn't we do that? Honestly, we just like torturing people like you. God's chosen little babies."

She hands him a notepad and a pen. He writes directions and draws a map.

"Thanks," says Cecily. "Don't bother calling the police. Mary, don't punch me. If I don't explain this, he won't get it and he'll call the cops."

"I understand," says Mary. "That last one was just borderline is all."

"Okay, so," says Cecily. "We aren't going to kill you; we're going to leave now. You have no idea who killed that guy, and thanks to my little toy, there will be no fingerprints. We have your wife and daughter. Your daughter went storming out of here, so we snatched her up, then we overheard your wife talking on the phone in the parking lot, so we snagged her too. If the cops show up, they all die. I can do a lot more with a lot less than just that little guy. Cool?"

Jay nods.

The women all exit except Cecily.

"I think," she says. "I'll leave that here for you to play with. Don't worry, it knows not to kill you."

As she leaves the church, she can hear Jay screaming for help and mercy.

Not praying, of course.

It would be silly to think God would help him right now. He's probably busy helping someone's favorite baseball team win a game or something.

CHAPTER
SEVEN

T he bank was equally the best spot in town and the worst. It had a couple nice concrete ledges for grinds, a sweet little grass gap, and a bank ramp around the back. It was basically a little street park.

The issue: cops patrolled it like crazy. Usually, a half hour is about all you're going to get before one of the tellers calls the cops. If the bank was closed, the security guy would call the cops faster. It was better to go when they were open. At least then the workers had better things to do.

The order is always the same; start out back where they definitely can't see you, go to the grass gap, then hit the ledges.

Billy rolled up the ramp and popped her deck into her right hand. She planted one foot on the ground and jumped into a 180. Picture perfect boneless and she could almost hear Dylan laughing. All Dylan cared about was modern flip tricks and street skating. The skating of the 80s and early 90s be damned. He wanted to be Koston, Reynolds, and Rowley. He didn't give a shit about what the Bones Brigade was doing.

Dylan kicks off and hits the ramp. When he rolls to a complete stop, he pops a smooth heel flip and rolls back down fakie.

He looks at Billy and winks.

Ethan shakes his head and rolls up the incline. He pops his deck up and pushes through the tough transition to get all four wheels on the wall. He pops off the wall and rolls down. He gets a little wobbly at the bottom but shrugs. He's counting it, anyway. He doesn't give a fuck.

Billy goes up next. She gets to the meeting of wall and ramp; she pops her board up as she jumps. She plants her front foot on the wall and pushes off, landing, and rolling away.

She rolls past Dylan and winks.

"Yeah?" Dylan says. "Watch this old school shit."

He rolls up the ramp and jumps off his board. He picks it up and flails it through the air like a baton. He slowly sets it down on the ground and jumps back on. When he jumps back on, the deck flies out from below him. He lands on his shoulder. He covers his face and shakes his head.

"Serves you right," says Billy. "Fucking dweeb."

"Yeah?" Dylan says. "I landed a tre over the gap last week!"

"Oh yeah. Sure. I believe that."

"I did! Ask Ethan."

"He definitely DID a tre over the gap," Ethan says. "The landing it part is up for debate."

"Man," Dylan says. "Y'all know damn well I'm lying. These fucking trucks couldn't handle it. I barely Ollie the fucker and feel the axle bend."

"I told you," Billy says. "Grind King is weak. Tensor would have been better."

"Yeah, well, sorry we don't all ride Powell and Independent."

"Look, they've been around forever and there's a reason, you know?"

This argument of old vs. new is always wearing Ethan out. He looks at his Blind deck. He feels stuck somewhere between Billy and Dylan in skating. He loves Jason Lee's Video Daze part, but he also digs Josh Kasper.

He rides Destructo trucks and Spitfire wheels because he didn't care. That's what came on the complete. Not having a local shop makes it easy to have too many options and not enough guidance on anything.

Either way, he's never noticed a difference between his set up and theirs enough to worry about it other than size. Billy rides an eight and Dylan rides a seven and a half. Ethan is right in the middle with a seven point seven five.

He has enough control on this deck, but it's not too bulky like Billy's. He doesn't know how she Ollies with that thing.

"You going to talk to Mooooooollllyyyyyyy," says Dylan. He's been unprovoked, so he must have gotten bored with Billy.

"No way," says Ethan. "Totally out of my league."

"She really is," says Billy.

"I think you should go for it," says Dylan. "What's it going to hurt? You've been crushing on her since freshman year. She's right in there.

Just go in and say, 'Hey, let's go get some pizza, then go back to my mom's house.'"

"Is that how you got Maria?" asks Billy.

"Fuck no! She would kick me in the nuts so hard they'd shoot out of my mouth and go golfing. I'd win the master's tournament."

Ethan was always nervous when they skated at the bank. Molly was one of the tellers inside. He knew that from bringing money for his mom's account. Each time he had to go to her window, he got so nervous. She was just barely an inch taller than five feet, but to Ethan, she towered over him. Her presence was terrifying to him. He thought of her so highly that she almost became a deity.

It was freshman year. Ethan's bus brought him to school at seven a.m. Classes didn't start until 8:30. He always sat in the cafeteria listening to music and reading either that month's Thrasher or Big Brother. This day it was Big Brother; he was reading an interview where the interviewer convinced Ted Nugent that the Insane Clown Posse had some sort of problem with him. It was all a button-pushing operation, and it was gold.

He was laughing to himself at the whole thing when a girl with brown hair tapped him on the shoulder. He turned around and saw it was Molly Goode. He jumped a little because why was she talking to him? He took off his headphones, and she asked what was so funny. He explained that the writers of a skateboard magazine were creating tensions between the Insane Clown Posse and Ted Nugent. She laughed a little and said both probably deserved it.

She stood there for a minute before going to the other side of the table and sitting across from him. She was the only one there that early, too. They talked about school and life for a half hour until her friends showed up and she sat with them.

That happened every morning for the rest of freshman year.

They weren't ever really close. They shared some classes together and always talked. At some point, Ethan developed a little crush on her. He loved the way she carried a book bag that was four sizes too big for her. He loved how her thick-framed glasses were always sliding off her nose. She always had a big smile and wave for Ethan when they passed in the hallway, and it started to be the highlight of his day.

Sophomore year, Dylan asked what the deal was. He says, "Are you ever going to ask that short girl out? She waves at you all the time. You talk to her in Science. What's the deal?"

Ethan tried to explain that he wanted to when they met freshman year, but she had a boyfriend. Then she didn't. Then she did again. Then she always seemed busy with softball and volleyball. He just never did. Time in high school flew by, and Ethan never had a real opportunity to try.

"Listen," Dylan says. "She looks like the girl from Scream's nerdy little sister. She won't be single for that long."

Dylan was right.

There was never a good time to ask her on a date.

Ethan spent his whole time in high school dating random girls he didn't have any interest in. It was so obvious he was uninterested he kept getting dumped. He even dated Billy for a bit when neither understood that platonic friendship was a thing. If you get along with a member of the opposite sex, and they like the same things as you, you gotta start planning that wedding. Both of their parents always asked about the future wedding. They would both laugh and shrug it off because neither of them even wanted that.

It didn't work out because all they did was skate together. They were friends. They both knew that. They both knew Billy was gay, and they were just doing what everyone around them wanted to do to get them to shut up.

Everyone except Dylan, who kept saying, "I don't get why you're dating Billy's gay ass."

Ethan didn't either.

One time, Ethan finally tried to kiss Billy. They both jumped back and away from the awkwardness. Billy said she thought she was gay. Ethan apologized for being that bad of a kisser. Billy said it wasn't his lack of ability so much as it was Beverly in Science class's overabundance of ability.

Life went on week after week for four years.

The goddamn monotony of life.

The three of them went to the gap next so that Dylan could try to land this three-sixty flip he was all about.

Ethan was being a little more realistic and trying to land a kickflip. He kept getting close, but every time he would either fall forward from the impact or get in his head and not try to catch the deck. He slammed hard on his last attempt and hit his head on the ground. He was thinking of giving it up then until a voice shouted, "Hey."

They all turn to see Molly standing at the bank's entrance. She's waving at them for attention, like they aren't already looking. "Oh," she says. "I guess you were already looking at me. My boss told me to come out here and make y'all leave. I don't care one way or another, I like watching from my office. But he's at the other end of my paycheck, so here I am playing security guard because my office is closest."

"Okay, sorry," says Ethan. "Wait... can I have one more try?"

Molly looks over her shoulder and then back at him.

She makes a hurry up motion.

Ethan kicks off. He tries to get out of his head for this one. He pops the tail, slides his front foot forward, he flicks his foot off the nose of his board. He watches as it flips under him, and he pushes his feet down as soon as he sees the bolts.

He lands four wheels down, both feet on the bolts. He rides away clean and up onto the sidewalk. He turns and blows Molly a kiss.

"Holy shit," says Dylan.

"Fuck..." says Billy. "Molly, sorry about the kiss thing there. I think he got a little TOO confident. I'll talk to him."

"Yeah," says Dylan. "Jesus Christ. Man was as nervous as a chicken smelling a BBQ five minutes ago."

Billy wants to say more to Molly, but she can see she's blushing, so she doesn't.

Ethan may have just called his shot, taken it, and made it.

CHAPTER EIGHT

"Your dad didn't give a shit that you took all of his stuff?" Dylan asks Billy. After the blown kiss incident, they went to Billy's house to find out if her dad had any idea about cleaning out that pool. He had a couple buckets of car cleaning supplies; weird little gift sets he gets for Christmas every year from Billy's grandma.

He also heard some rumors about what the pool was for. He heard it was half full of anointing oil and used for what the members called "healing." He heard from a co-worker that it was filled with holy water and blessed oils to keep some demon at bay. More than likely, he thought, it was just some weird Christian shit where they mixed a light oil with water.

Ethan asked Billy why she didn't bring up the fact that oil and water do not mix. Oil is denser. Just like all those elementary school projects, right?

Billy encouraged Ethan to go in and ask. She didn't want to hear about how the chlorine system wasn't even hooked up. The pool was just a giant bathtub. That's the one thing he apparently thought was a little fishy; why go to all the trouble to build a pool inside AND get the right equipment... but never hook it up?

Billy nodded along and said it did sort of sound like some weird cover up bullshit. But what would a church be covering up with a stupid pool?

Her mom started talking about the love *The Goonies* and maybe the church was hiding stolen money. "Remember that time you went to that weird church with Noah's ark?" she had asked. "They wanted people to sell their houses and give them the money!"

Billy sort of shrugged and didn't want to get into all that with her parents. They were disconnected at the best of times, but when there was a chance to talk about rumors or something, Billy had fucked up; they were chatty as can be. Never once had they asked about her college life; they didn't even ask if her telling them she had a girlfriend named Mandy meant she was dating a girl.

They didn't care.

They knew in a few years she'd be out of their hair for good.

Good for all involved, really. Billy was getting tired of playing the child to two people who were playing pretend parents. The whole thing was beyond her. She never noticed anything was weird about her relationship with her parents until she started getting older and noticed that everyone else's parents said things like, "I love you." She started noticing that maybe when Ethan's mom asks about his day, she wasn't just being nosey. When Dylan's dad tried to skate with them and fractured his tailbone, that was someone trying to build a relationship with their child.

Her environment was the opposite; it was that of the child who stayed past their welcome. She had been treated like she was twenty ever since she was seven. Walking home from school alone most days, cooking her own dinners if there was food in the house. Her parents weren't exactly mean or aggressive, they just didn't seem to give a fuck about what she did beyond the smallest little bit of playing a part.

She was ready to leave; they were ready for her to leave.

The worst part wasn't that she didn't think they would have a relationship anymore, it was that she didn't think she cared.

When her dad gave her the buckets, it was without question because he had no intention of ever using them. He would never give her something he planned to use. Giving her the supplies was easier than throwing them away or pretending to use them.

Win-win for her either way.

"Nah," she replies to Dylan. "You know how he is. He was just too lazy to throw them away."

"Maybe he thinks you're cleaning your car."

"What would he care? It's not like they bought it."

Her car was a gift from her uncle. An uncle she hasn't seen in the four years since he dropped off the car. Her parents were sort of the black sheep of their respective families. Her mother's older brother still tried to be involved in Billy's life to a point, and that point was four years ago when he dropped off a Ford Escort from sometime in the mid-seventies. He handed her the keys, hugged her, and said he'd see her next time.

Only there wasn't a next time. She had no explanation why either. One day he's visiting once or twice a month to see his sister, then all of a sudden, he won't answer his phone and the most her mom will say about the issue is, "you know how he can be."

More like how you can be, she had thought. Probably an argument that her mother is too goddamn stubborn to admit she's in the wrong about. That's usually how it goes. Her mother was intolerable to the other side of her family tree that they sprouted into a completely different forest and never returned. Billy was starting to realize her mother had some toxic traits around the age of thirteen, but what could she do? She was a kid; shouldn't her relatives try to help for her sake at least?

No, that's not how reality works. People are people and sometimes the awkwardness of sharing emotions can be a stronger border than any wall.

She had already made plans with Mandy to leave after college. They would settle down somewhere between here and Mandy's family. She couldn't abandon Ethan and Dylan. They were the closest thing she had ever had to family. Especially Ethan who had become a sort of annoying brother.

She hated how he felt about things. She could tell he was trying to cling onto something that he thought was slipping away. That wasn't the case at all. Billy had to make a life for herself. She couldn't stay here in this small town just because Ethan wanted her to.

If she did that, she would lose Mandy. Then what happens when Ethan gets married and settles down? Then who would she have?

She had to make sure she was building her own life while maintaining the parts of her old life that mattered. She would still call Ethan every day, she would still visit. Dylan was aware of this; he knew what change was. He seemed to register the idea that growing up doesn't necessarily mean growing apart. Maybe that was because he had his own plans with Maria, maybe that was because he didn't have a father who abandoned him and his mother with no explanation one day. She understood why Ethan felt she was abandoning him, she understood why he thought Dylan was too. She could only do so much for him though. And that so much didn't include staying behind in this place because he was too sad and afraid to leave it himself.

"You know," Ethan said. "Your dad might be right. It is pretty fucking weird that we didn't have to turn on anything and it just drained, like this was a hole."

"Wouldn't it have to go through the filtration?" Dylan asks, looking at Billy.

"Guys," Billy says. "Do I look like a pool boy? Do you see me hanging out with MILFs all day and getting laid for cleaning their pools? No. You don't. Because I don't know shit about pools."

Ethan and Dylan made eye contact and then went back to scrubbing. They knew not to fuck with her when the mood struck. When she got lost in her thoughts, she would bottle up all these feelings and lob them out like little hurtful word grenades. Neither wanted to fuck with that today.

They cleaned until the sun was setting. It started getting harder and harder to see when the shadows were in the room.

They had reached a point where they thought all they had to do was let it dry. They looked over the two plastic trash bins filled with shitty towels they bought at Walmart on sale for a buck each.

"What are we going to do with those?" Ethan asks.

"That's a problem for future us," Billy says while shaking up a can of black spray paint. She gets down in the pool and goes to the deep end. She spray paints two stick-figure-type skateboards running vertical in a line. Their wheels touching, nose and tail pointing out in opposite directions.

She paints two more exactly like them, running horizontal about a third of the way up from the bottom.

It forms an inverted cross made of skateboards.

She then sprays paints "Hail Skatan" above the cross.

"Fuck yeah," Dylan says.

CHAPTER NINE

Old buildings are creepy when they're empty, right? There's no way around it. Just a bunch of empty dark rooms. All made from materials by human hands. Just physical things.

Empty bricked-in structures. Wooden homes filled with dust. Each has darkened corners and too much silence.

Every house is haunted, and every building has a ghost. That's just how things are in the Midwest part of America. Too much time to sit around and make up stories for every bump and noise in the night. The five-hundred-year-old house is just as haunted as the school building built last year and every person who locks up a restaurant knows about the ghost inside.

A bank is no different. Stories of men dying during robberies, security guards who died on shift, or in this case; the little girl who got locked in the vault and suffocated.

It wasn't true, of course. It wasn't even possible. But that didn't mean that it wasn't the first thing Molly thought about on that one night of the week she had to lock up and leave last. She would walk by the vault, refusing to look in its direction but also tuning her ears toward it in case she could catch the sound of the girl crying. There would be no sound, the story was made up by her uncle Terry. Her father, Brent Beck, told her that Terry told everyone that, but it was a complete lie. Molly went one step further to look in the newspaper records from the year 1963, when it supposedly happened, but of course, found nothing.

"Goddamn you, Uncle Terry," she says to herself as she pushes a cart of empty cash drawers in front of the vault. The man has never been serious a day in his life and right now Molly wants him to bonk his little toe off the corner of a coffee table.

Maybe that's a little cruel.

But something.

Her dad told her that she had to get used to doing this. She would be doing it two nights a week when he retired, maybe five if Terry's son still didn't want anything to do with the bank. Damn kid was sort of lucky Terry and his wife split up. He had a whole other household; Molly was stuck in one that focused on the bank and only the bank. She would without question be alone here five nights a week.

She didn't want the responsibility of having a haunted bank to manage; maybe a regular bank would be alright, but definitely not a haunted one.

As she stacks the empty cash drawers in the storage room, she hears a click in the lobby like a door. She puts her hand in her pocket and comes out with her car keys. She finds the pepper spray attached to the lanyard and pokes her head out into the lobby.

"Hello?" she says. "Cindy? Did you forget something?"

No answer.

Had to be Cindy. She was the only other employee with a key. She was here earlier than her dad or uncle every day to get all the lights on and tills set up. She also couldn't hear a tractor trailer filled with dynamite crashing into a nuclear reactor. Had to be Cindy.

She goes back to cleaning up the drawers and trying to convince herself it had to be Cindy, when what definitely, without a doubt, no question about it, HAD to be Cindy let out a soft cry.

Molly closes her eyes and takes a deep breath. She doesn't need this shit. She didn't ask for this shit, and she can't handle this shit. She doesn't even watch haunted house movies. If there's one thing she's afraid of in the realm of the supernatural, it's ghosts.

She doesn't need to hear one crying.

Another soft whimper.

She shakes her head back and forth and silently mouths, "God-damn mother fucking ghost shit." She pokes her head back in the lobby and says, "Cindy? Are you hurt?" Again, no response.

She hears the sniffles of someone who is crying. Do ghosts have snot? Would their nose clog if they were crying?

"Is someone in here?" she says as she slowly steps out of the storage room and into the lobby. She hears the sound of a child crying. A low whimper.

It's coming from the vault.

Her brain races to try to remember what those things are. What are those things that people can create with their mind if they think about them enough? Did her fear accidentally create the vault ghost?

She feels her body start to shiver about the idea of being able to accidentally create ghosts. That happened once, right? What was the ghost's name? There was a government study she can't remember the name of.

She walks toward the vault and sees it's cracked open.

"Hello?" she asks cautiously. "Are you hurt?"

"Help me," says the voice of a child. "I fell asleep on a chair and when I woke up, it was dark. I panicked and ran in here because I thought it was the front door. I tripped and hurt my leg."

"You thought a vault was the front door?"

"I was groggy."

Molly shakes her head. Her fear turns into frustration. When she opens the vault, she sees a fully adult woman sitting on the ground counting money.

"What the-" is all she gets out before a hand spins her around.

"My, my," says the woman, holding her by her shoulders. "They really shouldn't leave a pretty thing like you in here all alone, should they?"

"Just take the money," Molly says. She knows not to play the hero. The cameras will pick up whoever this is and find them. They didn't even wear masks.

"It's not the money we want. We came for you."

Molly jerks her head back in confusion. She jerks it right back into the waiting arms of the woman in the vault. Her face is covered in a wet towel, and she feels herself getting heavier.

The last thing she sees before she passes out is the security camera walking across the front desk.

CHAPTER TEN

Ten in the morning is probably a little too early to be listening to Pennywise. It's the equivalent of chugging five energy drinks right as soon as your eyes open. Too fast, too early. Unfortunately, *Full Circle* was the only CD that Dylan and Billy could agree on.

The Offspring had annoying little brother vibes, Billy said.

AFI is way too sad this early, Dylan said.

Bad Religion is fucking lame, said Billy.

Hot Water Music is a little too slow, Dylan said.

NOFX is for thirteen-year-old boys who sneak their dad's Playboys into the bathroom, Billy said.

The last one had all three of them cracking up because they all agreed that, yeah, that's probably true.

Ethan just put the CD in and didn't even wait for a discussion. The pool was clean; it was dry, their work had paid off. *Why are we all standing around arguing over what to listen to?* He thought. The dumb little CD player probably won't even last an hour without new batteries.

"I think Dylan gets to go first," says Billy. "He's the reason we found it. Then Ethan, then me."

Dylan and Billy touch their fists together.

Dylan gets down into the shallow end and looks around. It's a dream come true. The deep end is fully skateable, and the shallow end is too if you don't mind powering through some tight transition. The coping even seems to grind just fine with a little wax.

He pushes off and rolls down the incline leading into the deep. He throws his weight around the corner, carving the pool with his face looking down. He pumps through the bottom to gain speed into the shallow. He powers through the tight wall in the shallow and kick turns frontside. He comes back and flows back into the deep for another carve.

When he's done, he just looks at Ethan and Billy. They all feel it. This is their special place. Nothing can ruin this for them.

Ethan goes next. He prefers carving frontside with his back to the bottom of the pool. He does a similar line as Dylan, only when he comes into the shallow the second time he tries to power up into the coping.

He can't get his legs and body right and he falls to his knees.

Billy skates faster and more powerfully than either of them. When she skates, it looks violent, like a fistfight. Ethan and Dylan know she's in her element here and she'll be the first to start hitting the coping.

Which is exactly what she does on her second carve in the deep end. She hits it frontside and slashes across the concrete. She powers out of it and speeds back over the roll in. She powers up into the right transition of the shallow end and slashes that coping too for good measure.

She's lost all speed from that one and steps off in the shallow instead of rolling down again.

"Can you fucking believe this?" Billy says.

They take turns ripping through the empty pool for the next half hour before taking a quick break to eat the sandwiches they brought.

"Dylan," Ethan says. "It's like eighty degrees. Why are you drinking chocolate milk? You're going to fucking ralph."

"It's all we had!" Dylan says. "I have some water for later, but I don't want to waste it."

"Whatever the fuck that means," Billy says.

They're finishing up their food when they hear wood crunching above them in the church. The sound is followed by four voices.

"Fuck," says Dylan. "My fucking dad..."

"That's your dad?" asks Billy.

"No, it's not my dad. He goes to the station that Glenn works at before work. I bet he fucking told Glenn about the pool."

"Goddamnit, Bruce," says Ethan.

They hear footsteps and four voices carrying down the stairwell. Obnoxious laughter and banging on the walls.

So much for their peaceful sanctuary.

"Holy shit!" says one of the four as he walks in the doorway. "We found some strangers!"

"Glenn," says Dylan. "This is our place."

"You can't share?" says the last of the four coming in the door.

Ethan, Dylan, and Billy actively avoid these four. The Markison twins; Matt and Ben, Glenn Hill, and of course, the ringleader himself; Marcus Rathorn. These guys are the worst stereotype of skateboarders; they're dirty, rude, loud, destructive, and violent.

"Haven't seen you guys around in a while," Marcus says. He's already shirtless, showing off the shitty tattoos he got in prison. He just got out last month and has already gotten into four fights and was put into jail for three of them. You would think going to prison for nearly killing someone in a fit of rage would make you rethink your violent tendencies. Not Marcus, he lives and breathes anger problems. The other three flock to him like sheep. They think his "don't give a fuck" attitude and violent nature make him cool.

It makes him a meathead jock with a skateboard and a bunch of mommy's money to build ramps at his shitty single-wide instead of fixing the floor that's falling in is what Billy and crew think.

"Yeah," says Ethan. "We tend to not want to skate places where we can be attacked by rats the size of Dobermans."

Marcus laughs at this and drops into the deep end.

He skates fast. A little faster than Billy, but not quite as powerful. The years of hard living have taken some of the muscle and strength from his body. Despite his appearance, he's not as strong as he used to be, and his legs can't power through transition like they used to.

Still, he was pro fifteen years ago, and it shows. He's already hitting the coping at both ends like it's nothing.

He pops out of the deep end and yells something incoherent.

Glenn is already switching out the CD for a *Slayer* CD.

What the fuck? Dylan thinks.

The four take over the pool and act like over-excited high school football players. They slap their boards against the coping, they chug beers, they throw cans on the ground.

They're here to party for one day, fuck the place up, and leave.

Billy's pissed.

She forces her way into the deep end and powers through the corners. She slashes coping in both ends. She pops out of the deep and Marcus winks at her.

"Love it when a babe is that powerful," Marcus says.

Billy doesn't react. She's used to this shit from the twins. They always say gross pervy shit to her that she ignores because they aren't even worth acknowledging. All four of these dudes live in one trailer together that may or may not have a shower. Life is already sneaking up on them to fuck them up, no one else needs to.

Ethan rolls in from the shallow and Glenn drops in. They pass each other and Ethan runs out of the deep.

"What the fuck, Glenn?" he says.

"Dude," Glenn says. "If you can't hang, don't skate."

Dylan shakes his head and sits down. He's not fucking with all of this. It'll work itself out when Billy gets irritated and tells them to fuck off and either; the four assholes fuck off, or they leave for the day.

Ben drops in and kick turns back and forth in the deep end. He doesn't even carve. Billy rolls her eyes. This behavior would be fine from anyone else, but these guys are assholes. They already barged in and ruined the overall vibe, now Ben is slowing them down majorly.

"Jesus Christ, Ben," Billy says. "Don't you have a fucking chicken shack to go clean at home or something?"

Rumor has it that the twins had cleaned out a few old chicken coops to live in. No electricity, no water, just hot in the summer, cold in the winter on a dirt floor with sleeping bags. What did they care, though? Being close to Marcus is what they wanted.

Billy drops in and carves around Ben. Ben jumps off his board and jogs into the shallow to get out. Billy carves for a bit before popping out again. She makes a face at Glenn and says, "errr, if you can't hang, don't skate."

Glenn flips her off.

Marcus is flying through the corners again. His trucks slapping the coping and sending chunks of concrete flying.

Billy drops in next; she's getting pissed.

She's skating faster than she has all day.

Glenn drops in and cuts her off. When she tries to turn, she moves at a bad angle and falls down the wall of the pool. She bangs her elbow on the spot she painted the cross and leaves a smear of blood behind.

She picks up her deck and throws it at Glenn as he carves. He falls too.

"What the fuck is your problem?" Glenn says.

"Wow," Billy says throwing her arms up. "I don't fucking know Glenn. You all show up, steal our pool, steal our CD player, and then try to kill us while we're skating. Fuck you. Fuck all four of you."

She storms out of the pool and Glenn follows her out of the shallow. They keep arguing the whole way.

"You gonna let that chick yell at you like that?" says Marcus.

Dylan stands up, he looks at Marcus and says, "eat shit."

He's flipped a switch in that primordial brain and Marcus is pissed. He comes storming over to Dylan with his body flexing. He grabs Dylan by the front of the shirt and pushes him back against a wall.

"HEY!" yells Matt. "Who the fuck is that?"

He points to the doorway where a woman is standing with her hands behind her back. She has long blonde hair and a smile.

Glenn and Billy were arguing right in front of her and didn't notice.

"Knock knock!" she says as she pulls a shotgun from behind her back and turns Glenn's head into a mist of blood, brain, and bone fragments with the pull of a trigger.

CHAPTER ELEVEN

He wakes up wearing a mask of dried blood.

Covered in small bleeding lacerations, his skin is no longer visible. Is it the red face of the devil or a man with severe head trauma?

His world is bleeding wounds and sliced-up thighs. He asks his father in the sky why he is letting this happen. Is this for the same reason Jesus was punished? He could live with that.

He watches the machine continue to spin and slash at everything in his office. It mangled his dead friend's body beyond recognition. Steven is behind Jay's desk looking like a pile of wet red clothes with bones.

Its bloodlust is insatiable.

Jay tries to stand. He places his hands on the ground and gets to one knee. The machine sees him. Its tentacled legs carry it over to him. It lashes out again and again with broken machinery. The cuts and slices on his hands this time.

In a moment of pain-fueled rage, he reaches out and manages to grab the thing. He throws it against a wall. It thuds and remains still on the ground.

He gets to his feet and stumbles to the couch. He falls into a sitting position. He runs his hands over his face and peels dried blood away from his nostrils so he can breathe. He can tell by the way it feels his face looks like tightly woven fabric. As sliced up as it can possibly be without killing him.

He sighs and lets his body rest for a second. The pain has been unending for the entire night. Every time he thought it was done, that little bastard started slashing again. At one point, one of the wires wrapped around the pinky of his right hand. It pulled it to the side until it broke and hung at a weird angle. As if that weren't bad enough, then the thing slashed the skin between all of his fingers.

He looks at the clock and sees it's ten in the morning. He's been stuck here with this thing for close to twenty hours. He suddenly feels an unending thirst. His stomach growls in hunger.

If he went to the door to try to escape, he was met with a small tornado of blades. The best thing he could do was lay there and pretend he had passed out. He did get some reprieve when the pain became too much, and he slipped into unconsciousness. That would always end quickly as the little thing seemed hellbent on making sure Jay was tortured forever.

At some point, he thought his mind had finally snapped.

Is this Hell?

Did I die?

Did I mess something up?

I'm sorry.

I'm so sorry.

He sits up, puts his feet beneath him, and stands. He walks to the small fridge and gets out a bottle of water. He drinks it in three gulps. Then does the same with another. He goes to his desk and picks up the phone.

The wires are cut.

Of course they are. If Jay knew anything about horror movies, it was that the phone lines were the first thing to go. Giving the tiny thing that much mental prowess may be a stretch, though. Jay thinks it's just because that pile of shit was born to destroy everything.

He takes in the state of his office.

Chairs slashed to pieces. The wall looks like it was attacked by an army of pissed off cats with swords. The carpet is covered in broken ornaments, dried blood, and chunks of the wall. His ceiling fan is still spinning, at least.

One of the blades has something hanging from it. Jay focuses on it and sees wires wrapping around it, as that little demon flies through the air like it's on a ride at the county fair.

The wires let go, and the thing comes flying toward him.

Jay lifts his arms to cover his face and feels all the wires wrap his wrists together.

This thing is just a ball of wires and pain. A tumbleweed of torment. A rubber band ball of agony.

This time, it locks his hands together and makes small slices on the tips of his fingers. He screams and tries to shake it off, but every time it starts to loosen up, the wires get tighter.

He can feel the blood circulation being cut off; this may be the moment he loses his hands.

He stands up and bashes the thing against the walls all over. He smashes it into a metal cabinet. He swings it through the air; blood sending strokes of color across the wall like the art of some demented painter.

He hits his shin on a coffee table and falls forward. He groans out in the silent agony that everyone knows accompanies hitting their shin.

His hands land on top of a pair of black boots. His eyes follow the boots up to a pair of jeans, past that to a black T-shirt. Above that is a face Jay recognizes, Daniel Berry.

Daniel steps on the thing attached to Jay's hands. He pries the wires apart with a knife he pulls from his boot. He slices the wires until all that's left is a pile of cut up wire.

"Thank you," Jay says as he finally feels he can stop worrying about dying.

"Don't thank me," Daniel says. "Thank God. Better pray too. We're going to need it."

Daniel steps past Jay. Two more sets of boots follow him into the office.

Jay rolls on his side and sees the three men looking around the office.

"There was only one," Jay says.

One of the men has bright red hair. For some reason this is comical to Jay all of a sudden. He starts laughing about how this huge man, muscles so big that the four X shirt he's wearing is still too tight, is so scary, but has this bright childlike hair. He starts laughing even harder because when did red hair become childlike in his mind?

"Is your name..." Jay says, choking on laughter. "Red?" He can't contain it. All the pain and misery flow out of his body in the form of laughter.

"Sure," the man says. "Call me whatever you want. My names Red now, boys."

"Isn't that a little mean?" asks the other huge man that isn't Daniel.

"I don't care. This guy has been pushed to his limits. He's a man of God. He's a carrier of the word. I'll answer to whatever he wants me to."

"Who am I, Preacher?" the not Daniel or Red asks Jay.

"Hmmmm," says Jay, laughing. "I don't have the energy for it. I need a nap. I need some food. There's a good Mexican place down the road. There's a waiter there named Craig. He's just this little high school guy. He's white as all get out; the other workers speak in Spanish a lot and he just shrugs. Always brings us Queso with our drinks. We don't even have to ask. I like Craig. You can be Craig."

"Craig it is."

Daniel and Craig help Jay up from the ground and set him on the sofa. Red brings him a bottle of water.

Jay drinks it in a few gulps again.

He's handed a Gatorade, and he chugs it. He starts to feel like himself a little now that he doesn't have to worry about a little yarn ball of death tormenting him.

"Jay," says Red. "Daniel is one of our men. He's been placed here to live so that he can keep an eye on the church. The church that those women are probably already at. He saw one of them in a gas station this morning and swore he saw your wife and daughter in their RV. Now we know this to be true."

"I am so confused," Jay says. "You just crammed the plot of fifteen movies into five seconds and expect me to keep up."

"There's something in that church that has to stay hidden from the world, Jay. Craig and I are the closest to your location. There will be more men on the way, but right now, we have to do what we can. Those women call themselves the daughters of Eve. Their leader uses Satanic black magic to manipulate electronic devices."

Jay looks at his hands and then shakes his head at Red. "Wow, that would have been nice to know yesterday morning," Jay says.

From behind Jay's desk, Steven's corpse rises to his feet. Wires flow in and out of his eyes and ears like worms. They crawl across his body like an infection.

"Craig," says Red, nodding at the corpse.

It walks toward them. Its fingers stretch until the bones break through the skin like talons. The man's teeth fall out and are replaced by pieces of broken motherboard. His eyes turn metallic. The thing opens its mouth and speaks, "prepare for salvation." The voice sounds like a sixteen-bit video game soundtrack. It repeats the line over and over as its appearance becomes more and more grotesque. It looks like a machine made of gore and broken bones.

"CRAIG!" Red yells.

"Oh!" Craig says, realizing he's being spoken too. "Forgot the new name."

Craig pulls a device from his back pocket that looks like a gun. When he shoots it, wires attach to the corpse. He pulls another trigger, and a pulse is sent through the body. The corpse collapses into a pile of gore and machinery.

"What do you think, Jay?" Red asks. "Will you join the Right Hand of Adam?"

CHAPTER TWELVE

Friendship doesn't mean the same thing to everyone. Sometimes it means a person you like to talk to, sometimes it's a person you share the same interests with. In Marcus' case, friendship equates to having his own personal gang. When someone fucks with someone in that gang, they need to learn that was a mistake. These people are his to beat the shit out of, not anyone else's.

Which is why, as soon as the gun went off, Marcus didn't hesitate. He dropped in on the deep end and powered over to the shallow where he popped out. What's the saying about as the crow flies? That's what his instincts told him. He could get to this woman faster if he went through the pool than around.

When he lands on the ground, he has his board in his hands, wielding it like a baseball bat. The woman sees him coming and tries to hurry up and reload. He's muttering insults under his breath. His fingers are getting splinters from the grip he has on the rough and jagged wood.

She can't move quickly enough.

Billy snaps out of her shock and kicks the woman in the kneecap; she saw a guy in a martial arts movie do that once and shatter someone's knee. In this case, it just made the woman drop the gun out of pure surprise.

Marcus swings hard and connects the metal of his trucks with the side of the woman's head. She falls down and Marcus swings again; this time, her nose and mouth erupt in blood. He swings three more times. Each time his skateboard comes up, it brings blood with it.

The woman lies motionless, her face a ruined mess.

Voices from upstairs start yelling for someone named Gail. Footsteps are heard running down the stairway. Billy acts fast and shuts the door to the room. She drops the metal bar in place to barricade it.

She looks at that for a second and thinks, *wait, why would that even be there?* Her thoughts are interrupted by the sound of bodies banging against the door.

"Gail?" says a voice on the other side of the door.

"If Gail is this dead bitch," says Marcus. "Her fucking face got smashed in after she shot my friend."

"Oh, no. Sweet Gail. I told her not to go by herself. She gets so excited."

"What the fuck is going on?"

"Right to the chase, huh? Ok. I admire that. There's a body of water in there, right? A little decorative pond, maybe a fish tank, it may be a hot tub for all I know. We just want to drain it. That's it. No biggie."

"What if it's already drained?" says Dylan, walking up to the door.

"Ohhhh, well, then we need to draw a cross on the spot it was and smear the blood of a virgin on it. Then we say, 'mortem ad patrem.' It'll start to glow, then we have to sacrifice the blood giver on the altar upstairs. Voila! Pretty simple, right? I can't believe I just explained that. I think honesty is the best policy, don't you? You already think we're insane people, I assume. If the shotgun blast and what you say are any indication, I could tell you there's a spaceship in there. So, yeah, cross, blood of a virgin, dead virgin."

All heads turn toward the spot Billy fell.

Sure enough, the cross is glowing a dark purple.

"Hey," says Billy. "I think your little spell fucked up! I got my blood on it, but I'm not a virgin."

"May want to reassess your definition of virgin, honey."

"I had sex with my first girlfriend when I was fifteen."

"Ah, so tell me this, you sound very feminine. You're a female, correct?"

"Yeah..."

"And you said girlfriend, so I'm going to guess you're a lesbian or bi?"

"Lesbian..."

"Now let me ask you this. The Bible was written by old men. These rituals were created by old men. Do you think these men would think you weren't a virgin anymore? Or do you think they made these rules thinking that the only way someone can have sex is in a man and woman kinda way?"

"Shit."

"Yeah, I don't dig the old ways either. Those guys are bastards. Absolute bastards. Did you know on the constitution there was a law that you could beat your wife as long as it was with a branch no bigger than your thumb?"

"Is that true?" asks another voice on the other side of the door.

"I don't know. I heard that somewhere. It checks out. Anyway, you know how it is right, sweetie? Men make the rules, they tell us to shut the fuck up, then if we don't, they throw us down and make us eat pig shit."

Marcus is searching the dead woman for bullets. He has a look in his eyes that says he's tired of all this jamming, and he wants to take care of business.

"What's your name?" asks the voice.

"Eat shit!" says Billy.

"I must have heard you wrong. It sounded like you told me to eat shit. But as I just explained, only a man would tell a woman that. And you, darling, would be very goddamn stupid to tell me to eat shit when I'm the one who's going to kill you. Keep that in mind. It can either be quick and painless, or I can use my machines to torture you for a week straight until your body can't take anymore. Totally up to you. So, I'm going to pretend I misheard, and you actually said... hmmm... what rhymes with eat shit... oh! Nice to meet you, Edith! I'm Cecily. I believe my friend Gail is in there?"

"Yeah, and she's fucking dead!" yells Marcus. He charges at the door like it's a person.

"What a shame. Still, we expected there may be casualties. We thought the Adams would be the problem though. Unless... are you an Adam?"

"No, I'm one pissed off mother fucker!"

"Definitely an Adam. Maybe not a registered one. Edith, you go ahead and come on out here. There are four of us. We can all go upstairs to the altar and take care of this. Then your abusive, angry father, boyfriend, whatever he is; he can leave with all of your friends."

"He's of no relation, family, or romantic to me. Lesbian, remember? We just went over this. He's an asshole."

"Take care of what, exactly?" says Ethan.

"Good question. I guess you'll just have to wait and see what Edith decides to do!"

"What if I hadn't been here?" asks Billy.

"Fuck! I'm tired of all of this backstory cramming. We have another Virgin. Some preacher's daughter. We were going to use her. Can we get the fuck on with this now?"

"Fuck you, you dried up old cunt," says Marcus.

"Nice! Wonderful! You're all too kind, really. I'll remember your kindness."

The footsteps go back upstairs.

"Fucking what now?" says Ben.

Dylan goes to the back door. When he touches the handle, it burns his hand and sends a sensation through his body like he's been struck by lightning.

"You'll not be able to leave until we figure this out one way or the other!" Cecily yells down the stairs. "It's all a waiting game now, friends. And I've got plenty of food and water up here. I can hang out for, gosh, a month if I have to!"

"I fucking hate that woman," says Dylan.

"Join the club," says Marcus.

CHAPTER THIRTEEN

How can anyone be having fun at a time like this? Carmen Barnett thinks. At first, Lisa was terrified. When their captors said neither of them would make it out alive, Lisa looked over at her mom and shrugged. It broke Carmen's heart. Not just because Lisa clearly didn't care about Carmen dying, but because she didn't care if she died.

"At least then I'll leave something behind," Lisa had said.

Carmen felt a dagger jamming into her heart and all the way out of her back. She couldn't believe her daughter could care so little about life. She put herself in her shoes; she tried to think about how the incident with Heath would make her feel.

She would be hurt. Who wouldn't? You put your love and trust in a person and start planning a future with them. You fall in love with them. You expect them to always be there for you. You know they will never hurt you. They're your protector. The pain that Lisa had to feel when Heath's actions shattered all of that.

But she would also understand that you can't ruin people's lives over one incident. Heath wasn't inherently bad; he was just a teenage boy. Teenage boys have a control issue. Hadn't she had to deal with the same shit from Jay? Boys will be boys. Why did Lisa expect Jay and Carmen to lose some of the most respected members of their congregation over a little lover's spat?

It was ridiculous, and Carmen agreed with Jay. It wasn't worth the hassle. Was it awful what happened? Yes. But what Lisa, Jay, Carmen, and Heath all needed to do was pray about it and really lean on Jesus.

That was the only way anyone's heart would mend. Heath and Lisa needed to pray together. They needed to be in contact with one another. They needed to fix the foundation that had been cracked in the building that was their relationship.

And this whole thing where Lisa wouldn't talk to Heath? So dramatic. Carmen wasn't going to tell Heath that Lisa wasn't home; what kind of example would she be setting as a mother?

Lisa and one of these women, Rhonda, were playing a card game and just having the time of their lives. There was alcohol involved. Carmen was hurt that her seventeen-year-old daughter was drinking like she had done it more than once before.

There was a knock at the door. The woman named Mary went and opened it. Carmen tried to listen to what was being said but couldn't make it out. There were two of the women in the RV with them, and another outside stationed as a sort of messenger between the group inside the church and the group outside. Carmen couldn't understand why Cecily kept saying they needed to do this, because the other five wouldn't be able to leave the church after they spilled Lisa's blood.

"Well," says Mary, leaning back in. "There's been a surprise. There's already a virgin in place inside. Cecily can't get out now until it's all taken care of. We lost Gail though." Mary ruffles Lisa's hair and says, "you're going to be alright, kid."

"Damn, I was really hoping I could prove to Cecily I belonged."

"Goddamn, Gail," says Rhonda. "I think you're going to be fine. Looks like a spot just opened up."

"You mean it?"

"I think when Cecily hears about all of... this..." she motions toward Carmen. "She'll agree."

A single tear rolls down Lisa's face. Her mother feels anger bubbling to the surface. It feels like the worst heartburn she's ever had, and she can feel herself starting to slip into it.

"Lisa," Carmen says. "You can't seriously be this stupid, can you? These... things... are going to take you straight to Hell with them. I wish you would come over here and pray with your mother."

The three others look at one another and start laughing.

"See," says Lisa. "A fucking prayer warrior! Got a problem? Just pray it away!" Lisa stands up and faces Carmen while she yells. With each word, she takes a step closer. "Broke your leg and can't go to cheer camp? PRAY IT AWAY! Can't find your car keys? PRAY IT AWAY! Your boyfriend beat the fuck out of you because you wouldn't let him fuck you in a porta potty? PRAY IT THE FUCK AWAY!"

When she yells the last, she hits Carmen with closed fists. Carmen covers her head with her arm, but Lisa keeps raining down blows like she's a monsoon in the Sahara and every bead of sand is begging for moisture. When she finally stops, she drops to the floor and starts crying. Carmen leans forward and holds her in her arms. She starts to pray.

Lisa jumps back and swings her right fist with all of her might. It connects with Carmen's nose and blood flies in an arch as her head whips back. Lisa is on her, instantly throwing more punches. She stops punching her mom and closes her hands around her throat, all while yelling, "PRAY IT AWAY!"

Rhonda and Mary stand in the background, all smiles and pride.

Lisa stands up and brushes herself off. Speckles of blood cover her clothing. "Fuck you, mom," she says. "And most importantly, fuck your god."

Carmen begins sobbing. She balls herself up as tightly as she can to get away from the knowledge of what just happened here.

The moment of silence is broken by a gunshot. The women look at each other in confusion. The RV door flies open, and Deanna comes stumbling in. Her right shoulder is bleeding.

"Fuckers shot me!" she yells.

Another gunshot goes off and a hole appears in the side of the RV.

"Looks like your dad's here," Mary says to Lisa.

In the back of the RV, through the window in the room she's been locked in, Molly watches four men run down a hill carrying weapons.

She can see them and she's hoping they can't see her. The way they started shooting, it looks like they aren't taking captives.

CHAPTER FOURTEEN

Hair on grip tape is one of the oddest sensations. It doesn't really hurt, and it doesn't hurt. It's somewhere between annoying and painful. When trapped in a room with nothing but concrete, sometimes all you have for a pillow is your skateboard. You lay your head down and think, *well this isn't all together pleasant, or unpleasant really.*

Billy tries to nap, but she can't get past the spurt of violence, and the fact that two people are arguing about decks not even a half hour after said violence.

"All of that shit is for kids," says Marcus.

"Dude," says Dylan. "Just because it isn't fucking flaming death skull from beyond death and bad assery, doesn't mean it isn't good."

"No, it means it's being influenced by the children's toy markets. How many of those skinny ass little boards do you go through a month?"

"Yeah, okay, so this is actually my second deck in like three months. Seriously, they don't break THAT easy."

"I bet I could break that thing with one swing on the ground. You're relying on landing on the bolts every single time. It's unrealistic. Especially in a pool."

"Why does that matter?" asks Ethan.

"Because if you're in a pool you need a lot more control," says Billy. "That's why Dylan always looks like he's about to start duck walking and quack his head open."

"Yeah," says Matt. "Stop riding little pussy ass toothpicks. Grow the fuck up."

"Alright," says Billy, standing up. "All of that was unnecessary. Sexism aside, no one even acknowledged my joke."

"It wasn't funny," says Ben. "You made a duck joke."

Billy looks around the sliding door for a way out. She hits the glass with her board, and it just bounces back.

"Yep," she says. "It's official. Weird force field shit."

"You guys ever see Alan Peterson's part in It Is 'What It Is'?" asks Matt.

"Yeah," says Billy. "One of my favorite videos as a whole."

"There's that scene they spliced in. You know what I'm talking about? Where the mouse is in that snake's tank? It gets bit and the snake just sort of stalks it, right?"

"The fucking circle of life, dog," says Ben.

Marcus is helping Billy try to find a way out. He touches the door and pulls his hand away in a hurry. It was like touching a stove.

"What do you think?" Billy asks.

"Sorta, kinda think we're fucked," says Marcus.

"Same. Maybe we can fight off those four."

"Not if they have guns like that one did. We're lucky she wasn't a faster reload."

"Dude," yells Dylan. "You've got to be fucking kidding me! Yeah, 'Right' is a way better video than 'Baker Bootleg'."

"No," says Matt. "No way in Hell. 'Baker Bootleg' has Reynolds, Santos, Greco. Fuck, even Tony Hawk shows up!"

"I wonder how much they had to pay that fucking sellout."

"You know," says Ethan. "I don't know why everyone is so Hell bent on calling him a sellout. What's he supposed to do? Tell people to NOT like him?"

"The fucking video games!" yells Ben. "Ever since those games came out, now we've got all of this corporate involvement in skateboarding. It wasn't Rob or Bam that brought Nike in. It was Tony Hawk."

"Don't even get me started on those two. Remember when Bam's video parts used to be actual skating instead of jumping into bushes?"

"Doesn't matter, 'Label Kills' is the better video."

Billy shakes her head at Marcus.

"The kids are at it again," he says.

Billy walks over to the door on the other side of the room and puts her ear to it. She can hear talking from upstairs, but not close. As she's listening, the voices grow louder until the one who talked before is yelling down the stairs.

"Hey," Cecily yells down the stairwell. "Can we talk?"

"No!" yells Billy.

"That's a shame. Hold on, I'll write it down."

A few minutes later a sheet of folded paper is slid under the doorway. Marcus picks it up and unfolds it. A pile of dust falls from the paper.

"It's blank," Marcus says.

The dust floats over to the portable CD player. It goes into the two speakers in the front of the device.

Slayer starts playing before it distorts and plays in reverse.

"Oh fuck," says Billy.

The CD player explodes in a pile of parts. All the parts start weaving together and forming legs underneath the main part of the device. It stands on wire tentacles that are attached to the speakers to give it balance. Something purple glows from the slots the speakers came from. The top of the player opens, and the CD inside starts spinning as it's lifted into the air by another tentacle like wire. It wields the CD like a blade.

Matt doesn't think or plan. He runs forward and swings his skateboard at the thing. Mid swing, the CD connects with the middle of the board and slices it in half.

Matt falls backward and crawls on his ass as the blade moves toward him. The thing runs on two legs, pushing the CD across the ground like a lawnmower, and Matt is the spot it's missed for three weeks.

Ben moves quick to try to help Matt, but he stops halfway and grabs his stomach.

When he got close enough, the thing slashed the CD at him so fast it was barely noticeable.

Ben wobbles on his feet as blood pours from the wound. He holds the skin tight, thinking it's like a movie and his insides could fall out.

The machine stops its chase of Matt and focuses on Ben. It slices at his head one time before going after Matt again. Ben reaches for his ears like he's got a headache. The top portion of his head slides away from the bottom and his body hits the ground at the same time as half of his head.

Marcus grabs Dylan's skateboard from him and moves quickly to the machine. When he's there, he slams the steel on the underside of the board against the concrete on the lip of the pool. A loud crunching sound and he's pulling the hanger, or long metal part connecting the two wheels, from the rest of the truck. Now the kingpin is exposed and looking like a painful way to go. It's a solid steel bar that a bolt goes over to hold the truck together, only now it stands alone like a dagger.

Matt screams as the CD slices half of his left foot off. It uses the CD like a shovel and throws the half of a foot across the room. It moves again but freezes in midair. The CD stops spinning and it twitches.

Marcus helps Matt stand as they run away from the machine.

The machine shakes as the metal rod Marcus jammed into it is buried in its mainframe. It collapses to the ground and falls apart.

"I told you those Grind Kings would break," says Billy, not knowing what else to say about what just happened.

Matt tries to sit up to see his foot but instead gags and throws up. Marcus is busy wrapping his own shirt around the wound as tightly as he can.

Matt is going to bleed out if something doesn't happen, Marcus thinks.

Behind them, they hear the familiar sounds of metal, plastic, and wire slapping together.

When they turn to look, Ben's body is standing again.

Wires move like worms and seal the wound in his stomach. The plastic frame of the CD player is placed on top of his head like a helmet to hold on to anything that didn't fall out.

The CD is attached to wires that emerge from the top of his plastic helmet like the light of an anglerfish. His skin peels back from his mouth and fingernails. His teeth are exposed, and his nails look like talons.

The light display from the player is in place of one of his eyes. It glows purple.

Ben takes a step forward, and the CD starts spinning. A voice comes from the speakers that have been sewn over his ears and says, "I am the way. Prepare for salvation." It repeats the phrase over and over again.

Marcus tries to lift Matt up, but he can't move fast enough. The new Ben steps on Matt's groin with all of its weight, and a loud popping can be heard. Matt cries out in agony before the CD slashes down and slits his throat all the way to the bone. Marcus turns to run.

Dylan and Billy are heading to the Women's shower with Marcus and Ethan right behind them when what used to be Ben slithers between them and rises to full height.

This transformation took no time at all, just milliseconds. It separates Ethan and Marcus from Dylan and Billy. Marcus waves the other two off. No sense in four dying instead of two.

The used-to-be-Ben is now standing every bit of eight feet high. It looks like all of his bones and insides have been sealed together and stretched to make a sort of giant human snake.

When the thing opens its mouth, wires shoot out and wrap around Ethan's leg. He's thrown across the room and hits the wall in the deep end of the pool.

Before he slips into unconsciousness, he sees someone shooting the massive Cobra Ben with what looks like a taser.

He'll worry about that when he wakes up, though.

CHAPTER FIFTEEN

Having a teenage daughter was a lot more work than Jay thought it would be. He thought she would always be Daddy's girl. She would always watch football with him on Sundays between church services. She would always play softball. She would always be his best friend.

Wrong, wrong, wrong.

At fourteen, this weird thing started happening with Lisa. She started to make other friends; she took up cheerleading; she didn't want to spend as much time with old dad as she did her friends at the mall.

She always needed Dad's credit cards though, so that was some sort of reliance for Jay.

He thought about all the good memories, all the bad ones; you can't have one side of the coin without the other and they're all just as important. The time Lisa made him a custom "world's greatest dad" shirt at the mall means just as much to him as the time he caught her smoking cigarettes at fifteen with the neighbor kids.

He couldn't think of the good love, without the tough love he had to dish out to protect her from the evils of the world. The substances. The bad habits. The boys who only want one thing.

The Heaths.

When it came right down to the teeth, skin, sweat, and shame of it all; he knew he was wrong. He let his fear of failing God and church stop him from protecting his daughter. He expected her to accept this one bad thing as a way to show him how much she loved her dad.

It shouldn't be that way in his mind. He knows it now, and he knew it then.

When he gets Lisa and Carmen away from this insanity, some changes need to be made. No more being a pushover and walking mat for the church. No more selling out his family for the fake positivity of the majority.

"Hey!" he yells, grabbing the barrel of the rifle. It burns his skin, and he jerks away. "Don't fucking shoot at the RV! They could be in there, you idiot." He slaps Keith hard across the face and the big man looks at him as if trying to figure out where this bravery came from.

"I see you're feeling up to task," says Red.

If they knew what Jay's mind was doing, they wouldn't have handed him a rifle. His brain is telling him to kill everything that walks or stops him from getting to his wife and daughter.

"Check it, three o'clock," Daniel says.

A woman is creeping through the darkened woods toward them. She must have snuck out and come around the back of the RV.

She moves as quietly as can be. She's holding a giant fuck you type knife in front of her and angled directly at the group.

The woman notices that the men see her, and she freezes on the spot. She turns and runs down the hill as fast as she can.

She isn't fast enough or slick enough to outsmart Jay fucking Barnett. The man who has bagged the biggest buck every year for five years running.

He lines up the shot. He pulls the trigger.

The woman's head jerks back, and she falls forward.

The men move down the hill toward her quietly. They don't want to alert the others that the gunshot connected.

Red aims at the RV door in case one of them puts two and two together and tries to come out, guns blazing.

Jay thinks that's a bit overkill. If they had guns, surely this woman would have had one.

When they reach the body, they can see the bullet hole. It's on the left side of her neck, just barely above where the back connects.

It may have scraped her spine.

She lay there rolling around trying to speak, but all that happens is more blood pours out of the wound.

Jay takes the toe of his boot and pushes it into the wound. He twists it further.

The woman fumbles with her jacket and pulls out a walkie. She tries to talk into it, but her voice won't let her.

The walkie buzzes with another voice. "Rhonda? Rhonda, are you ok?"

Daniel picks up the device and speaks into it, "She's not alright at all. She'll be dead soon. Give us the women you took, and we'll be on our way. You stole a preacher's-"

"Respira vitam, machina Satanae," the voice says, cutting him off.

The plastic casing of the walkie splits and electrical wires wrap around Daniels' face like an octopus hunting prey. He screams and tries to pull it from his face, but it doesn't do any good.

The other three men join in and try to pry the device away, and it won't give one bit.

"Sorry, brother," says Red, before shooting the device with his rifle.

Blood, bone, plastic, small electronics, and brain slap against the tree behind Daniel. He falls to his knees and then finally face-down.

"I should have known," says Red. "Witchcraft."

"Witchcraft?!" yells Jay. "That was a kid's walkie-talkie that just did that. It just latched onto Daniel's face like it was a goddamn tick!"

Jay grabs Red by the collar of his shirt and shoves him against a tree. He puts the rifle under his chin and grits his teeth.

"You just killed him," Jay says. His finger gets heavier by the second.

"Hey," says Keith. "He had to do it. That was Witchcraft. Your friend was gone anyway. Let's put the gun down."

Red just stares Jay in the eye, as if challenging him to go ahead and blow his brains out.

Jay thinks to himself how lucky he would be to be Daniel right now. Currently, Jay knows his wife and daughter are trapped in an RV with women who can turn toys into death machines. He would be better off facing God himself at the pearly gates. He isn't equipped for this.

He slowly releases Red.

Red brushes his shoulders off and says, "We good?"

Jay nods.

Jay turns his head fast to the left. His ears picked up the movement of multiple people. But no one is around.

"Ah, fuck," says Keith.

Jay and Red look toward him and see he's motioning to an empty ground where two bodies were lying not even three minutes ago.

Above them, they hear something climbing through the tree limbs. They see small flashes of white mottled skin. They hear groans of pain and pleasure.

The rustling stops.

A speck of blood drops down onto Keith's shoulder from the trees above.

"Nope," Keith says as he moves to stand by Jay and Red. "I've seen enough movies to know that's when something snatches me up into the trees.

They see a white creature moving down the tree. It looks like a spider covered in human skin. Two arms and two legs on each side climb down the tree as if it were the most comfortable spider to exist. It moves behind two trees that grew close together.

A woman's hand grips the side of the tree and a face peeks around.

It's the woman they shot.

It moves back into hiding when it's been spotted.

"Hey," says Jay. He's nodding at a foot that's not hidden behind the tree. On the top of the foot is a black cross. It looks like the absence of matter, in contrast to the pale skin it sits upon. "Daniel got that tattoo two weeks after he got saved."

The three men pull their guns up and prepare for a fight.

The woman's head pokes out again and makes a sound like a whimper. Red wastes no time and takes a shot. It misses and blows bark from the side of the tree.

The woman laughs and then moans right after. The moan sounds orgasmic.

It moves like a flash of light from behind the trees and pins Keith to the ground. Jay and Red start shooting and reloading as Keith screams below the thing's assault.

It's the two bodies of Rhonda and Daniel. They've fused together where Daniel's head used to be. The two bodies are connected by wires and small electronic pieces. It moves like a spider, all the arms and legs functioning as legs.

It stomps and punches Keith all over. He rolls and dodges some blows but rolls right into others.

Jay steps up and places the rifle at the side of the thing's head. It turns and screams at him before one of the hands grabs his testicles and squeezes.

He goes to his knees in agony. The creature stands to full height above him. Its head twitching back and forth from the lust to kill flowing through its body. It's foaming at the mouth and moaning like it's in the middle of an orgy.

The knife Rhonda was carrying is jammed into the side of the thing's head, and it stops moving completely. A wire pierces its skull, shooting sparks and mist. All of its weight crashes down on Jay and he has a hard time breathing. He crawls out from under the thing and sees Red helping Keith sit down.

"Thanks, Red," Jay says.

"It was me, you stupid fucker," says Keith.

"Thanks, Keith."

They hear screaming from the RV and the slamming of a door.

One woman is dragging Lisa toward the church by her hair while another stands in the doorway with a gun to Carmen's head.

"You want your wife's head to not look like oatmeal, you better fucking come out!" yells the woman holding Carmen.

"Goddamnit," says Red. "Let's go."

He nods to Keith.

Keith nods and moves slowly and painfully in the opposite direction to try to set up a flank.

Jay watches as his daughter is dragged into the church.

He hopes and prays he can take her fishing after all of this is done.

CHAPTER SIXTEEN

The sound of a bullet hitting the thin wall of an RV was all the sign that Molly needed to know it was time to hit the fucking road. She waited around, thinking something would eventually happen to either let her know it was time, or to let her know it was time to get her ass in gear. A bullet hitting the place you're finding safety in is probably the closest thing the universe is going to give you to shit or get off the pot. Whatever the fuck that means, she just hears her dad say it when they're driving, and a car won't decide to go into the left or right lane.

She looked out the back window and couldn't see a thing. She heard the women in the front shuffling around and trying to figure out what the Hell was going on.

"I'll go out," she hears one of them say. "I can go out the side and take the knife."

Molly thinks about a side exit for a minute and then hears a door close basically right beside the door to the room she's trapped in.

She searches the room for anything that could possibly be used as a weapon. She finds a small screwdriver and shrugs.

It'll stab, she thinks.

She stabs the screwdriver through the thin door and works it around, stretching out a hole in the material.

She squats down to look through the hole but stops herself. She's seen enough Lucio Fulci movies to know this would be the scene where she takes a fingernail into the eyeball all the way up to the knuckle.

She backs away a few feet and then squats to look. She can't see anything because the front door is open, blocking the rest of the RV.

She feels relief. She can get out of that side door, and no one will notice because they're too focused on whatever is happening outside.

She manages to get a hole big enough to get her fingers through and flip the lock.

She opens the door and takes one step out. The security camera from the bank turns and looks at her from the ground. It looks like a camera on two legs. It stands and starts flashing her with a light from the lens. This must be their plan; the little fucker would flash like a siren.

She picks it up and goes into the door across the hall from her escape route.

She's inside the small bathroom of the RV with the only light coming from the flashing of this camera. It looks like the world's smallest rave for the world's loneliest girl.

She finds a light switch and turns it on. She feels something stab at her ankle. When she looks down, she sees the camera-wielding a little sewing needle like a sword and jabbing at her jeans. She kicks it into the shower stall and goes for the door.

The thing is already flashing its light again. She's going to have to get rid of it.

She opens the small cabinet beside the shower and finds a book bag. Inside the bag are all these devices that look like tasers or something. They're made like handguns with a wire where the barrel would be. At the end of the wire is a thin needle, almost a sewing needle.

She looks down at the camera and it's picking up the same kind of needle to try to stab her again.

She points the device at the camera and pulls the trigger. The needle pierces into the lens. Steam and sparks pour out of it as it collapses to the ground, lifeless.

She zips the bag closed and throws it across her shoulders.

She opens the door and peaks out. She hears one of the women say "Rhonda?" like she's talking on a phone.

She heads out the side door and runs as fast as she can through the woods. She heads away from the chaos as fast as she can until she hears screaming at the church.

Goddamnit, she thinks. *Am I really about to be THAT person?*

She grunts, looking back and forth between freedom and the church. She starts toward the church when she hears more screams and gunfire from the direction she was calling freedom.

Good fucking call here, Molly, she thinks.

She gets to the church and sees through the windows of a sliding glass door some sort of half man half robot, all fucked up and scary, swinging a blade around.

The four people inside run one way but are separated by this giant pale snake. It shoots wires from its oddly human-looking mouth that wrap around one of the poor soul's legs and throws him into what looks like an empty swimming pool.

Holy shit, she thinks. *That was Ethan!*

She slides the door open, runs as fast as she can to the weird ass snake and shoots the wire into it. It starts with mist and sparking like the camera did.

The device gets too hot, and she throws it to the ground. The snake slowly slithers away behind the other thing. This one is gnarly. It's got a CD player for a head and razor-sharp talons. She tells the man holding a skateboard to take one of the guns from her backpack and shoot the thing. He does it without hesitation and there are more sparks and mist.

This one crumpled up and crawls on top of the snake. They both stop moving and appear to be lifeless.

"And who the fuck are you?" Marcus asks.

"Molly, I think I was supposed to be like a virgin sacrifice or something. I don't know. I didn't stick around to get all the details. Let's get Ethan."

Dylan and Billy come out of the shower room and poke their heads around the corner.

"You guys get the fuck back in there!" yells Marcus. "I can get him."

He slides down into the deep end of the pool and throws Ethan over his shoulder. He takes a small run up one wall and then runs over the roll into the deeper end. He sets Ethan on the lip of the pool and gets out.

Molly shakes Ethan. He starts to open his eyes.

"Wake up, stupid fucker," she says as she slaps him hard across the face.

"Damn it," says Marcus. "Let's get to the locked room first before you beat his ass."

Ethan comes to enough that he starts standing on his own and rubbing his head.

"The fuck is that?" Ethan says as his eyes open wide enough that his eyelids are at risk of folding into his skull.

"Fuck me," says Marcus, looking at the thing between them and the shower room.

It's both creatures mangled into one absurdity of flesh and machinations. It has electrical wire weaving in and out of its overstuffed body like someone's grandma went on a Four Loko bender before sewing up a teddy bear. The CD player sits in the spot where its right eye would be. Its body is like a massive slug; long, fat, and serpentine-like. The CD hung from its mouth by a wire. It breathed in and shot it in their direction.

If the thing's aim wasn't shit, it could have taken a head off. In the end, all it got was a deep laceration on Marcus' right shoulder.

"Go to the other room," Marcus says, nodding to the other shower room. "It's too fucking stupid to realize there are two. Take my deck. It's behind you."

Molly turns and picks up a skateboard. It's chipped and worn out.

"Take that to the fucking Grind King," Marcus says before running toward the creature and distracting it.

Molly helps Ethan move as quickly as he can into the other shower room.

She holds the door open for Marcus, hoping he can make it.

He shoots the thing with the wire gun; it stumbles and rolls into the shallow end of the pool. Marcus holds the trigger until the heat burns his skin so deeply he can't feel it.

He screams out and lets go of the trigger.

He motions for Molly to throw him another one.

As he reaches to catch it, wires pierce his skull. They look like massive snakes moving through his body. The gun hits his hand and flies into a wall.

Marcus falls to the ground and digs at his skin with his nails, trying to pull the wires from under his skin. It's no use. They continue to travel along his skeleton and nervous system, taking over his body completely.

He makes eye contact with Molly and shakes his head.

She closes the door just as the massive slug slides back out of the pool.

CHAPTER SEVENTEEN

A muddy hill in flat boating shoes is a recipe for a broken ankle. One small slip in mud, one little puddle. It's all over. Jay wishes he would have thought in the long term and not the short term and gone home for some shoes and a change of clothes because these khakis aren't doing it either.

"Nice to see you," says a woman holding a gun to Carmen's head. She points it at the back of Carmen's right shoulder and pulls the trigger. The sound of the gunshot is drowned out by Carmen's cries and pleas for mercy.

"What the fuck?" Jay yells moving forward. His approach is stopped when the woman puts the barrel of the gun back on Carmen's head.

"Now we're even. You shot me, I shot her. My name's Deanna. You're Jay, he's someone, and this guy..." she turns and shoots Keith through his eye from one hundred feet away without hesitation. "Isn't going to be much help for you anymore. Now, sweet little Carmen is absolutely dying to get away from us. I think if I turn her loose, she'll run as fast as-"

"Distraction," says Red, leveling his gun at Deanna. "She's doing this to buy time so they can kill your daughter."

"Oh," says Deanna. "Figured that one out, didn't he? Anyway, which one is it going to be, Jay?"

"Me or Red?" Jay asks, not fully understanding the situation at hand.

"Fucking idiot," says Deanna. "Your wife or daughter. Fucking red head shit, the bed is right, we stand here talking long enough; your daughter is dead and Cecily wins. Tough break for the world, really. Or you shoot me, I kill Carmen, and you can save your daughter, the world, the whole fucking thing."

Jay lifts his gun to point at Deanna.

Carmen's eyes go wide and she's shaking her head. She's mumbling a million miles per hour under the tape across her mouth. Probably pleading not to die.

But even God had to make a sacrifice to save humanity, Jay thinks.

He pulls the trigger.

Just a hair before he pulled his trigger, Deanna pulled hers. Blood and bone shoots from the side of Carmen's head at the same time both explode from the back of Deanna's head.

Both bodies fall to the ground lifeless. They're stacked and tangled like two lovers.

Jay bends down and apologizes to his wife. He says a quick prayer to his father in heaven before standing up and looking at Red with anger.

"I didn't choose this," Red says. "Remember that. I'm here to stop whatever is happening."

"Understood," Jay says. He stifles the urge to shoot Red for the fun of it. "Which way?"

"I think going in the front is asking for our heads to get caved in. So, let's go around back. There has to be an entrance, right?"

They find the sliding glass door and enter the basement.

The sound of polyurethane wheels rolling across concrete can be heard like a wind chime on a silent night. In the deep end of the pool, a man is rolling back and forth on his skateboard.

The man is huge, and he's wearing a white sheet over his head and body. Two blackened eyeballs are in the front where a face should be. Some kid's version of a skateboarding ghost.

He goes up, comes down.

Goes up, comes down.

Back and forth without turning.

Both men turn to leave the basement, but the sliding door won't open now and the touch of it feels like touching the surface of a grill that's been on all night.

"Interesting," says Red. "I didn't know how it would be possible to allow people in but not out."

Up and down.

Back and forth.

The ghost has an almost hypnotic quality for Jay as he just stares at it.

Jay is nudged on his shoulder by Red. Red walks to the pool and points a gun at the skateboarding ghost.

"Hey," he says. "Knock it off or I'll fucking shoot."

The ghost turns for the first time and rides the board seemingly into the air. It uses the skateboard to slap the gun from Red's hand before landing back in the pool and resuming its back and forth. The gun skids along the concrete. Red pulls out his taser-like device and points it toward the ghost.

Red watches as the ghost turns and heads into the shallow before carving around the small inclines fast. It heads back down into the deep and flies above Red. It holds the nose of the board as it lets the tail slap the coping right where Red's foot is.

Red feels his bones shatter as he falls.

His leg dangles into the pool as he screams out in shock. The ghost is in the air again; this time landing its tail on Red's kneecap as it's placed on the coping.

Red rolls over and motions for Jay to help. Jay can only see the door at the front of the room standing open. A wooden block has been removed from a locking device.

Jay runs away from the sounds of Red's body making gushing and crunching sounds as a skateboard slaps him all over his body.

When Jay makes it to the door, the one woman that dragged Lisa by her hair is standing there. Jay instinctively shoots; the bullet hitting the woman right in her throat.

He can see two more women with guns turn the corner into the basement. He tries to duck and hide in what appears to be a side bathroom. He slams his body against the door until it opens. A kid is standing there, and he says, "Sorry, we didn't know there were two of you." Jay nods at the kid. He looks through a crack in the door and can see the thing still launching into the air and landing on Red's corpse, making a further mess. Red has now become a part of the concrete.

This whole operation went to shit, Jay thinks. I would have been better off alone.

At this point, Jay's mind has decided that he will do whatever he has to do to get his daughter back.

May God have mercy on the rest.

CHAPTER EIGHTEEN

"So..." says Jay. "What's the... plan?"

Ethan shrugs and sits back against the wall.

"I assume my dad will send out the search party. Oh, probably around an hour ago," says Molley. "Until then, I guess we guard ourselves with those gun things."

"Well, hopefully, it goes better for that group than my little group of four people. Who, by the way, were armed and ready. Also, with 'those little gun things.' Supposedly, they shoot an electric pulse that fries the electronics and a splash of holy water to kill the demon."

"My dad's a banker."

"Let's hope he doesn't come here. I don't think they need a loan."

Jay jumps up along the wall and manages to hook his fingers on the lip of the concrete separating the two rooms.

"Whose hand is that?" says Dylan.

"Fuck!" Jay yells as he drops back to the ground.

"Will the deck Marcus give me fit through that hole?"

"Yeah, people are over there," says Ethan. "It's my friends Billy and Dylan. They can hear us. They don't have a way out either. Just sit down and chill for a bit. I don't think it will, Dylan."

"No can do. They've got my daughter."

"Go ahead and go back out there, then. I'm sure it'll be okay."

"Yeah, sure. I could make a run for that stairwell."

"Stairwell?"

"There's a door and a set of stairs."

"Shit. Was it open?"

"Yeah, unless the women with guns I saw stepping through are holograms of some sort."

"In that case, it probably won't be long before those crazy asses are pounding down the doors."

Jay punches the wall and sits down under one of the sinks.

"Hey, Ethan," says Dylan from the next room. "Who has it worse? Us or Colby Dotson?"

"Colby. Hands down."

"Who's that? I recognize the name," says Molly.

"He went to school with us all the way up until sophomore year. His dad owned that exotic fish store in town."

"Oh yeah," says Jay. "I bought a lizard from there. It was so cool. I had it in my office. I took it for walks on a little leash. Got loose one day and ran under the stage at church. May still be there."

"Is that that mega church fucker?" asks Dylan from the other side of the wall.

"You betcha," says Molly.

"Dude," says Billy. "You're a dick!"

Jay just shakes his head. He hears this shit all the time from young people who haven't found God.

"You wouldn't let anyone from The Cliffs sleep in your mega church last summer, remember that?"

"They had other places they could go," Jay says in defense.

"You have a massive AIR-CONDITIONED church. Why wouldn't you just let these poor people whose apartment building burnt to the ground in the middle of fucking July sleep in a pew or something?"

"They weren't members."

"See, total dick."

Jay feels eyes digging into him. He looks at Molly and sees she's staring at him with the anger of a million newly orphaned baby birds after a deforestation effort happened to open up a spot for a mall.

He shrugs and closes his eyes.

"What happened to Colby?" Molly asks.

"Oh!" says Ethan. "His dad had that store, right? Well, one night UPS or whatever took a shipment of piranhas to his house and not the store. His dad rigged up the bathtub for the night to keep them. He didn't tell Colby. Colby comes strolling in first thing in the morning and steps into the tub. He thinks his little sister must not have pulled the plug. So, he squats down to pull it but starts getting attacked. He fell forward and got torn to shreds. Apparently, he can't talk or anything after the fact and refuses to go to school."

"Fuck. That had to be awful."

"Tell her about lizard man!" yells Dylan.

"Okay, so it gets worse," says Ethan. "He was so pissed at his dad that he decided to kill him. But his brain was all warped and wonky, so he gets it in his head he's a supervillain like in a comic book. He goes to his dad's store and gets all the lizards. Puts them in a cardboard box. Horrible idea because some of them don't get along. So, he's carrying this box, with some lizards inside killing each other. All he cares about is the visual of him opening his dad's bedroom door and letting the lizards run free before he attacks him. He doesn't make it that far because some guy walking his dog sees him and asks what in the flying fuck is going on. Colby explains the whole thing. Says he's going to eat his dad and lay eggs. Weird shit. Total villain monologue. Guy says 'okkkkkk' then calls the cops. Cops roll up and see Colby trying to wrangle all these lizards. He's got bite marks all over him and he's just genuinely not doing so hot. Anyway, he starts spitting at the cops and saying his saliva is acid. The cops lit him up, and he ended up looking like Swiss cheese."

"This has to be a story someone made up," Molly says.

"Good luck explaining that to these two," says Billy. "I've tried to tell them one million times it doesn't make sense. The news would have shown that. People would STILL be talking about it. But these two are fucking idiots."

They sit and bathe in their own thoughts for a half hour or so. No one wants to talk; they're all talked out. They're just waiting on the metaphorical shit to hit the great big metaphorical fan at this point.

Jay looks at the door as if he telepathically knew it was about to be knocked on.

"Hey, friends," says Cecily.

"Oh, fuck off," says Ethan.

"Nice to speak with you, too! My girls, which there are only four of us now, thank you very much, are helping this blob become a little more efficient. We have an idea. See, no matter how strong a door's lock is, it's not going to hold against the weight of five people, is it? No. No, it probably won't. We know we can get in the other door and get little miss. We can. If we HAVE to do it that way, it's going to be bad. We're talking violence unlike anything you've seen- "

"I don't know," says Molly. "I've seen some wild shit in the past couple hours. Gonna be hard to top."

"What if I make your brain feel like it's coated in fire ants? What if every bone in your body starts shattering and piercing your skin?"

"Yeah, that would suck pretty hard," says Ethan.

"Good, we're understanding each other. There's a hard way, which isn't that hard for us, just for you. It's the annoyance for me. And then there's an easy way. Pastor Jay, how badly do you want your daughter safe and sound?"

Jay stands up. His lip twisting in anger.

"Your silence tells a story. Here's the scoop. I know for a fact there is someone in there with you that the someone I want would do anything for. Bring him outside, then you can have your daughter. Easy peasy lemon cheesy? Or is it squeezy?"

"It's squeezy! And Jay isn't going to do that, he's a pastor," says Ethan. He doesn't finish or start his next sentence because the barrel of a gun is shoved in his face.

"Maybe I am kind of a dick," says Jay as he forces Ethan and Molly to the door.

CHAPTER NINETEEN

Thud, thud, thud go Ethan's shins as he's dragged up the stairs.

They're letting Molly walk, cool as a cucumber, just walking up the stairs like nothing is happening.

When they get to the top, he's tossed into the sanctuary. It's been empty for so long he can see the dust sitting in the pews. It's so thick the red fabric looks slightly brown.

They point to one of the front pews and Molly sits down.

Ethan, however, is thrown to the front where his ribs land on the wooden altar.

"Fuck," he says. "Why are you treating ME like shit but not Molly?"

He feels the heel of a shoe on his thigh, digging in, causing his leg to cramp. He screams out and rolls on the ground.

"You're a real fucking idiot, you know?" says a woman's voice that isn't Cecily. "We want her to think about joining us. We want you to bleed out on the altar like a stuck fucking pig as an example for all men."

The woman kicks him in the groin before walking away.

"Brittany," says Cecily almost in a warning. "We don't need to kill him before we get what we want."

A woman sits beside Molly.

"I'm Beth!" the woman says. "Nice to meet you! I think you're a part of the crew now, girlie."

"No thanks. I think I'd rather not drive around in an RV killing people like some weird Texas Chainsaw Massacre family."

"See," says another woman. "I told you, Eliza. It looks like part two!"

"No one cares. Just because we drive an RV. Also, that movie only has one single scene in a food truck!"

"Our leader even has superpowers, sorta!"

"At what point in any of those movies do they have superpowers?" says Cecily. "So, drop it."

Cecily helps Ethan stand and sets him in the pew next to Molly.

"You see," Cecily says, speaking to Molly. "I've been left with the three newest members of my little family. They're passionate, yes. But also, a little raw around the edges. Two of them bicker like children and one of them is always mad. I'm hoping you can balance that and be my right hand, you know?"

"Yeah," Ethan says with a smirk. "You need a right hand when all you do is jack off all day."

Cecily punches him hard in the jaw. He falls down into the pew.

"Sorry, Molly," Ethan says. "Not my usual kind of joke or insult. But I saw an opportunity, and I took it."

"Understandable," says Molly.

"Where's my fucking daughter," says Jay. He's been standing in front of the baptismal tub staring at the crucifix this whole time. "I haven't said a single word because that was the deal. I didn't think I needed to ask."

"Jay," says Cecily. "Sweet, sweet little Jay. Your daughter is here. She's locked up in a coat closet at the front entrance. I will personally let her out and dust her off as soon as we get the girl we want.

"Her name is Wilma," says Ethan. "But she goes by Billy because Wilma is a granny's name. I think if you're wanting to kill her, you should know her name. Marcus, Matt, Ben, and Glenn. Those are the names of the other people you killed. And whoever the fuck that was with Jay. But considering his attitude right now, I don't much care about his feelings."

"His name was Red," says Jay. "Then there was Keith and Daniel. Keith wasn't his real name, and neither was Red. I think they let me make up codenames or something. Real military nuts, you could tell. Are we just going to sit around here fucking waiting? Or can we be a little proactive?"

Cecily walks to the stairset and looks down.

"Right about now," Cecily says. "Some of my crafts should be waiting."

"You're going to kill them down there?"

"No, they know to injure and maim. Not kill. It'll be okay, trust me. Wait, why am I telling you to trust me? You need to sit down and shut the fuck up. I think when you agreed to my deal, it made me feel some sort of kinship with you. The duality of man, I suppose."

She walks to Jay and grabs him by his hair. He tries to fight her off and lands a solid backhand on the tip of her nose. The strike just further enrages her, and she slams his face into the side of the tub.

"What would you do for your god?" she whispers in his ear. "Would you clean his feet? Would you let him eat your only source of food? Would you let him piss on you?"

Jay just breathes deep through his broken nose, trying desperately to get some air into his lungs.

"What do you think?" Cecily continues. "Do you think your prayers are more important than the mother who has breast cancer? Do you think it's completely normal that God punished humanity, and then punished his own son to make up for that? He's a cruel and sick being, Jay. But as cruel and sick as he is, you're going to find out I'm much worse if you don't start playing by my rules. You don't make the demands. I let you slip a little there. But it's time for a reminder, don't you think?"

She forces Jay to his feet and sits him on the side of the tub.

"Let me see your hand," she says as she takes his right hand in hers. She caresses it in a motherly way as if Jay has just had an accident and needs soothed.

She grabs his ring finger and, in a flash, snaps it back until it's lying flat on the top of his hand.

Jay screams out and tries to get away. She holds on to his hand and squeezes the broken finger at the joint. She grabs his pinky and twists it three hundred and sixty degrees. The bones can be heard crunching like the changing of gears on a bicycle.

She finally let him go.

He crawls into a sitting position and holds his hand close to his chest.

"Forget about the Old Testament," Cecily says. "I am the way. Not your shriveled-up old man and his son with his stupid little holes."

She looks at Ethan.

Ethan's blood runs cold as a small smirk crosses her face.

"Remember this," she says in his direction.

Cecily stands up and places her foot on the back of Jay's foot. She slowly puts more and more of her body weight upon it until Jay begins to moan louder and louder.

She smiles at Ethan and backs off.

"I don't give a fuck about your suffering," she says.

"Don't worry, Molly," Ethan says. "I'll get us out of here."

"You don't have to do that," Molly says. "The whole tough guy, savior thing. I figure Billy is the only chance we have of getting out of here."

"Me too. Me too."

A loud crash followed by screaming and more crashes erupt from below.

"Ah," says Cecily. "My favorite song. Violence."

CHAPTER TWENTY

Billy can't imagine a worst-case scenario than accidentally becoming a virgin sacrifice. Just sorta stumbled into it, too. How does that happen? Is that the shit people dealt with when human sacrifice was the norm? Two out of three steps into the role without even realizing it happened.

What a crock of shit.

These things should come with warning labels. "DANGER! You've just completed one out of three steps to become a virgin sacrifice!"

Life isn't that nice though, is it?

Dylan is standing at the door to the shower room. He's empty-handed because Marcus smashed the shit out of his deck. Either way, they have to go next door for those weird taser things Molly mentioned; he can grab the deck, Marcus left him then.

"You ready?" he asks Billy.

"No," she says.

He opens the door. Billy lunges out, swinging her skateboard, but nothing is there. Just an eerie silence.

They shrug and move over to the other room. Billy grabs the book bag filled with weapons. Dylan picks up Marcus' deck and hefts it in his hands while fighting back tears.

"You know," Dylan says. "I never did like that guy."

"I know," says Billy. "I know."

Billy rubs Dylan's shoulder while he takes in the new emotions for what they are, a milkshake made of broken glass. He feels them bubbling up through his body in a wave of emotional pain and overload. He feels tears run down his cheek and hears Molly sniff some back in.

He sniffs his nose and nods his head.

There's something out there this time.

In the deep end of the pool, the ghost is back. Riding back and forth like it was before.

Up and down.

Down and up.

"Couldn't it at least do a kick turn or something?" Dylan says.

He pulls out one of the tasers and shoots it into the deep end at the ghost. The ghost decides to do a kick turn then and carves around the deep end to avoid the wire.

"Fuckin' Bob Burnquist over here, apparently."

Billy walks up to the deep end as the ghost starts to roll back and forth again. She throws her deck in its path and causes the ghost to fall to the ground.

It jumps up fast and high. It lands in front of them and stands completely still.

A red stain flows down the white sheet like a trail is being formed. When it reaches the bottom, a dribble of snot, blood, and saliva drips to the ground in a long elastic string.

It shuffles toward them like it just figured out it has legs. The sound of bones grinding together is so loud it could be a power sander.

Dylan moves forward and hits it in the face with the top of his deck. A new red spot spreads where the nose should be.

It continues shuffling along like the walking dead in a Romero flick.

Billy shoots it and the wire sticks to the fabric. No help in any way.

"Fuck this," Billy says. She throws her board under her feet and skates past the ghost. As she passes, she grabs the sheet and pulls it off the thing.

It's skeletal at best. The skin has been pulled so tightly to the body it looks like a glove. All the organs create bulges in the skin. The top of the head is gone. In its place, a pile of wires writhes around like a bowl full of worms.

Dylan shoots it in the head. Sparks and mist pour out of the head as the wires stop moving and the thing falls forward. He has to let go of the trigger because the device is getting too hot.

Billy starts swinging her deck in huge arches smashing into the wires. They right and try to escape, but with each blow, more and more of them stop moving. The thing curls up into a ball and holds one arm out as if begging for help before Dylan pulls the trigger again.

All the wires stop moving, the limbs go limp, and the thing makes a sound like a computer powering down.

"That was a little too easy, in my opinion," says Dylan.

They turn to see four more monstrosities drop from the ceiling above and block their way upstairs.

"What the fuck..." says Dylan.

The four creatures before them look like someone's idea of Robo-Cop after eating mushrooms.

Tentacles where arms should be digital readouts where eyes should sit in a skull that is now made of contorting wires and broken pieces of skateboards.

Three stand vaguely humanoid, while one looks like a spider made out of the arms of the dead bodies. The arms fuse into Dylan's skateboard, where the digital display of the CD player now sits.

"Aren't we done with that thing?" Dylan says as he steps forward and slams his new skateboard into the top of the CD player. The parts that fly from it are absorbed by the three humanoid monstrosities that are advancing on him.

He stomps his foot through the thing, sending the skateboard to the ground. His foot breaks through it and he stumbles backwards.

"Ok," Dylan says. "Marcus was right. That thing was weak."

Billy shoots the spider thing with her wire-gun. The same sparks and must shoot out of it and it lays down motionless.

The other three move quickly and try to surround them. Their bodies are that of a human turned inside out and held together by electrical wire. Their spines look like motherboards controlling their bodies.

Dylan shoots one, it goes down lifeless almost immediately.

One reaches out for Billy; she ducks and clocks it in the head with her deck. When she moves to swing again, she's embraced around her waist by the other.

"Move your head!" yells Dylan. He swings his deck full force. It connects with the thing's head and bends it backwards from the spine. It releases Billy as its head now starts fusing into its back to create some new abomination.

Billy shoots the one that fell. It sizzles and remains motionless.

She feels the weight of another human being hit her in the back and she falls down face first.

"Holy shit," says Dylan.

Both roll over and see that the last thing has molded into itself to create a pile of gore from the remaining bodies. Tentacles fly in every direction, some end in razor-sharp bones while others end in pieces of broken skateboard. It slaps together two tentacles that have merged with the trucks of a discarded skateboard. It creates the effect of two hammers slamming together.

Billy shoots the thing with a new wire-gun. It takes the blow like nothing as the sizzle immediately fades into nothing.

Dylan sighs and says, "I may die right here. It's entirely possible." He charges toward the two hammer tentacles with two of the wire-guns. He takes a blow to his shoulder from one but manages to grab them both. He wraps the wires tightly around the trucks, making them tied tightly together. The whole time, the other tentacles are slashing and hitting him. He feels one slice across his shoulder blade, deeper and more jagged than the rest, and falls into the mass. His hand tries to find something to grip on the pile of torn meat. He puts his hand on a bone and starts to push his face out of the thing's mass. He can feel his air being sucked from his body as the thing tries to absorb him.

He feels something pull hard on the back of his shirt and he's falling back to the ground beside Billy.

"Thank you," he says before grabbing another wire-gun from her bag and shooting the wires he has tied together.

The thing instantly deflates; blood, bone, metal, machinery, and wood flow across the ground like it came from a clogged drain.

"You're going to probably have a disease," Billy says.

"None worse than I got from Ethan's mom," Dylan says.

"He's not even here to defend his mom's honor."

They jerk their heads upwards as the sound of gunfire comes from the floor above like thunder.

"Hopefully he's able to up there," Dylan says as he picks up his new and Marcus' old skateboard.

Together, they make their way up the stairwell.

CHAPTER TWENTY-ONE

Secrets are nice to have when they benefit you in a situation. Something you have in your deck, that no one else does. They don't know about it either, so when it's all stacked against you, you break out the secret and win it all. Kind of like a small handgun tucked into Jay's sock. Small enough to kill at close range, small enough to not be seen. His good friend, the NAA-22S, is nuzzled right up above his ankle bone, held by a small strap. It keeps his leg warm, and his soul feeling safe. He never tells anyone it's there; they'll never notice the small lump through his jeans. So, he's always had his good friend there with him.

The handgun was a gift from a friend. A man who spent a tour in Iraq; A man who is still there, actually. He handed Jay the gun at a church-sponsored BBQ and says, "Keep this on you, you know, just in case." Jay was afraid of the man. He had shown signs of violent behavior at church and Jay thought this was maybe his way of telling him to be on the lookout for himself.

Jay was itching to get a hold of it. He had loaded all six shots before he left the house yesterday morning. He's always afraid of someone shooting up the place they all settle on to eat. The way these terrorist threats have been for the past few years since 9/11; he isn't taking any chances.

He didn't expect the terrorists to be a bunch of twenty- to fifty-year-old women of all different backgrounds traveling in an RV. That's the kind of thing you only see in movies. Even then, they're usually hippies or cheerleaders. He had to figure out his next plan of action.

The woman named Brittany is his biggest threat next to Cecily. He can see it in her eyes. She could be just as cruel, but her anger wouldn't let her stop. If Cecily hadn't stepped in a little while ago, Jay knows the outcome would have been worse. She has a look in her eyes like a lion waiting on its prey, but also that of a coyote without a pack. She's ready to lash out and attack anything that gets in her path. Jay plans to stay as clear of that path as possible.

She's too far away to grab, anyway. If he goes to her, Cecily will know something is up.

Beth is sitting by those worthless kids, so she's out. Eliza is pretty close, sitting on the altar. It's not like he can't move around freely. He could get to Cecily if he wanted, but truth be told he's a little, no make that a lot, afraid of her.

A lot afraid of Brittany too, if he's being honest with himself. These other two seem childish. Like they haven't realized how serious what they're doing is. Or maybe they're possessed.

He doesn't think he could get behind Cecily and pull the trigger without her realizing he's there and fucking him up. The same could be said for Brittany. Eliza or Beth, it is. Or he could use both to show how serious he is. He just wants his daughter. That's it. They can do whatever else they want. He knows whatever they're trying to do here, God will stop it.

He moves around the chapel like he's taking in the scenery. He can't move too far toward the front or Cecily will beat his ass for trying to jump the line. He can tell she's on high alert, anyway. Something about those kids.

Beth and Eliza conveniently meet up by the pulpit and start chatting about something. They don't know that this conversation has helped Jay in so many ways.

He waits until no one is paying attention and pulls his buddy from its spot. He points it at the back of Beth's head and pulls the trigger.

The shot is loud in the silence, but not as loud as Eliza's screams as blood splatters her face.

Jay acts quick and wraps his free hand in Eliza's hair. It tangles and creates painful knots. He pulls her closer to him. Her hair feels like a rope tied tightly to the neck of a bull. Jay uses all the strength he can muster to make sure she screams out in pain and fear.

He points the gun at the air and shoots again as a warning for Cecily and Brittany to not come close. When he points the gun at Eliza's head, everyone is staring at him, confused.

"I want my daughter, and I want my daughter right FUCKING NOW!" Foam pours from his mouth as he screams. He's dehydrated, hurt, and pissed off. His pride feels a little bit kicked to shit, too.

"Jay," says Cecily. "You were going to get your daughter. Free and clear. Notice I said, 'you were?' Yeah, that's because I think that now that has changed. I think now we'll keep her and break every bone in your body. WERE."

"Yeah? Go ahead and fucking try it!"

He grinds the barrel of the small six-shot handgun into Eliza's head. He doesn't see Eliza drop a wristwatch from her hand.

The watch quietly breaks apart; tiny gears and machinery going into the hole in Beth's head. It all moves like an army of bugs.

"What do you hope will happen here?" Cecily says. "Do you think that now we're just going to let you both go? Even if you get your daughter out of here, we'll hunt you both down."

"Not if I kill every single one of you."

"There are still three of us and just one of you. Even if you kill Eliza; Brittany and I are the ones you need to worry about here. Sorry, Eliza."

"It's ok," says Eliza. "I'm still learning the ways of Eve. I understand what you mean."

"Nice family bonding moment here," says Ethan. They all look at him like they forgot he was sitting there with Molly. "Actually, go ahead and forget I'm here. We don't have a horse in this race."

"Cecily," Jay says. "Give me my daughter. We'll leave and you can do whatever."

"Yeah," says Cecily. "Maybe I should just eliminate some of the equation."

Cecily goes to the doors at the front of the sanctuary and opens one. Lisa comes running out of the door and straight to Jay. Her face is covered in tears, snot, and fear.

She wraps her arms around Jay's waist and squeezes against him.

"I'm so sorry, Dad," she says choking on tears. "I'm so sorry."

"It's okay, honey," Jay says. "We're getting out of here right now."

He doesn't move the pistol from Eliza's head. He kicks the back of her foot, telling her to walk.

"You'll get her back when we leave," Jay says, walking by Cecily and Brittany.

"Sorry, dad," Lisa says releasing her grip. "But we aren't going anywhere."

Jay turns to ask what the fuck exactly Lisa is talking about, but his voice is cut off by Lisa jamming a small pocket knife into his side.

He pulls the trigger out of reflex. Eliza doesn't have a second to process her death before it's over.

He shoots two rounds toward Brittany and Cecily as they duck and run between some of the pews.

Lisa tries to run, but her head is jerked back hard by her hair. Jay swings her by her hair and slams her into the side of a pew. He can feel the air leaving her body. He feels a rage greater than anything he's ever felt. His own daughter; a shit sucking Satan worshipper.

"You fucking jezebel!" he screams. "I knew there was something wrong with you the very second you crawled out of your mother. You're not my daughter. You're a curse I've been made to carry for seventeen years. You've become my cross to carry. I thought to myself, sure, father and daughter survived the cult massacre. We would be made. The church would be made. The news would come flying in and we'd be so fucking rich we couldn't stand it."

He points the gun at Lisa's head. He's frothing at the mouth again; his anger has become physical. He feels like his insides are turning to lava. Every single muscle in his body is tense.

"I guess," he says through gritted teeth. "A man losing his wife AND daughter to a cult is a little better for me, isn't it?"

Behind him, he hears the podium get smashed. He turns to look and sees Beth's reanimated corpse. She's nearly doubled in size; her body is covered in skin that's been stretched to its limit and about to burst from the new muscles and machinery coursing around. The watch face sits nicely in the wound Jay's bullet left behind just above her nose. Her nails have grown into thick talons made of bone.

He feels a pain in his groin and falls to his knees. He looks up to see Lisa ducking behind one of the pews.

"Goddamnit!" he screams.

He turns to face the new monstrosity in time to see Billy and Dylan walk in the doorway. Billy shoots the thing with the wire-gun, and it pauses for a second before ripping it free.

"Ah, damn it," says Dylan. "We're going to have to cross streams!"

Molly and Ethan stand up and get wire-guns from Billy.

Good, Jay thinks. Let them deal with that thing. *I've got my own problems to worry about.*

CHAPTER TWENTY-TWO

Ethan looks at his friends emerging from the doorway and breathes sighs of disappointment, relief, and oh shit, now we're all gonna die together, at the exact same time. *Why didn't they just hide forever?* He thinks. That wouldn't make sense in the long run at all. They'd eventually have to leave or starve to death. And Cecily was telling the truth about them having food. That woman who sat by Molly smelled like pizza somehow.

He watches as this new monstrosity doesn't bend or budge to what has happened. It took the shot from the wire-gun and kept on going like nothing ever happened. *Damn shame too,* Ethan thinks, *would be nice if something were easy.* That's never the case, though, is it? When things are bad, they get even worse until the universe snaps and has to start over at not bad. It's a whole thing and anyone who's been alive for more than fourteen years knows it.

He grabs a wire-gun from the bag that Billy has, Molly does the same. They don't even pay any attention to all the screaming in the background. What's the point?

The thing jumps up onto the crucifix and hangs by one hand latched onto Jesus' face like a face hugger from Alien. It's long nails digging into the side of the wood. A purple line comes from the watch face and lines up on Ethan's shoulder. Without thinking, he dives. So does everyone else. Luckily, they make the right call as bits of bone and teeth fly out of the creature's mouth like bullets from an Ak47. Pieces of the stage break off; sawdust fills the air from the wood below.

Ethan feels pain in his thigh and sure enough, when it's bad it only gets worse: he has three holes in a perfect line. The weird thing is they're all sealed, like whatever entered was hot enough to burn the nerves and seal the wound.

They all hide behind a piano and a small wooden wall covered in carpet to hide from the laser targeting of bloated flesh bag robo machine of death. Molly tears off a strip of her jeans and uses it as a makeshift bandage around Ethan's leg.

"It honestly doesn't even hurt right now," he says. "I think it's adrenaline, or it went in so clean."

"Either way," Molly starts to talk as more bones and teeth hit against the piano like its target practice. "We need to make sure if it does start bleeding badly, you don't die."

"Here's my idea," Dylan says. "The three of us run in different directions, so it starts shooting. Then, when we all have our wires locked into its skin, Ethan can shoot it from back here with two. Sound good?"

They all nod.

Dylan takes off almost immediately, he knocks over a blood-covered Cecily in his travels and heads to the back of the church, yelling, "RoboCop is shit!"

Molly and Billy take this as their cue and run in different directions toward the side of the church. They both run fast and dodge whenever the purple line is near them.

A line of holes appears in the wall behind Billy. She keeps running and dives behind a pew. She lands in a puddle of blood and rolls under more pews, so she doesn't have to think about that.

Molly jumps behind another small wall on the other side of the stage and shoots at the thing. Her shot pierces it right below its ear and she yells, "I'm set!"

Dylan runs toward the thing as it's shooting pews. It's too focused on Billy to notice that he's not even a foot away and got his shot clean, too. He pulls the trigger, and it pierces the thing's thigh. He dives behind a pew and yells, "I was aiming for the face! Holy shit, I'm a bad shot!"

Billy rolls all the way to the last pew and turns into an army crawl facing the thing. Its light is trying to find where the last shot came from, with no luck.

She watches as two more wires pierce the creature in its chest. She sees Ethan duck behind the piano.

She takes her shot and hits the creature in its shoulder.

"Now!" she yells and all four of them pull their triggers. The thing shakes as steam pours from every part of its body. Electrical sparks fly around like lightning bugs as it collapses to the ground.

It looks like a deflated skin balloon when it finally stops moving.

Billy breathes out a sigh of relief but doesn't get to enjoy it. She's pulled out from under the pew by her hair and thrown hard. She flies through the air like she was launched from a cannon and lands in the baptismal tub. She tries to stand but slips on the bottom. The tub is already filled with water, and it's gotten cold.

The crucifix falls over from the impact and lands on the now-dead creature, sending blood into the air like a fine mist.

"I've had about e-fucking-nough of this," says Cecily. She marches to the tub on a mission.

Dylan tries to tackle her, but she palms the top of his head like a basketball and chucks him into a wall. Molly runs from the side and tries to grab her legs. She's kicked in the ribs for her trouble and hears a crack that's followed by immense pain. Ethan pushes the piano toward her, the wheels rolling over the carpet. Cecily backhands the piano and sends it flying toward the back of the church.

She grabs Ethan by his throat as he falls and holds him to her face.

"How the fuck are you all of a sudden Superman?" Ethan asks.

Cecily smiles, showing a mouthful of wires moving like worms over teeth made of metal.

"Oh, that explains it," Ethan says.

Billy finally gets her feet placed in the tub and jumps out. She charges Cecily and punches her in the face. Cecily throws Ethan back toward where he started. She grabs Billy by the hair and drags her back to the tub.

She says nothing as she forces Billy's head under the water and pins it below her foot.

CHAPTER
TWENTY-THREE

A few minutes earlier:

Cecily looks at the bullet hole in her arm and shakes her head. The pain is real, concrete, explicit. To her, it's more of an annoyance than anything. She had everything laid out perfectly. This proves it. She knew that girl would come charging in for the rescue. She could have been one of Cecily's. She absolutely has what it takes to be her second. The same can be said for little Lisa. She's mad, calculated, cruel, and sick of being bent to the will of the world.

Brittany is the same, but she needs her temper controlled. Too many years being told she has the wrong skin color and too many years seeing people that look like her treated like shit by society. Cecily understands and loves her like a twin sister. But still, the anger from all of those years bubbles over into a lava flow of violence. She's done well to keep it in with Cecily's help, but realistically a person can only take so much before they want to see the world feel the same pain they've felt all of their life.

Cecily looks over at Brittany. She's already scrambling to the end of the aisle to attack Jay. Cecily grabs her ankle and stops her. Brittany may be the most brutal and violent person in the room, but Jay still has a gun.

"Brittany," Cecily whispers. "Be careful. He still has a gun. Ours are at the front still." She thinks about the two fully loaded rifles sitting by the tub. She kicks herself for not hiding them all over this room. But everything was fine. She didn't need a backup plan until now.

"Look," Brittany says nodding. "That's clearly a six shooter. He shot Beth and Eliza, shot one into the roof, then the two over there. He has one bullet. That's it. We can make him miss."

Cecily kisses Brittany's head and holds her closely. "I love you, Brittany," she says. "When this is over, we have to protect Lisa."

Brittany nods in agreement and kisses Cecily deeply.

They break apart and use the commotion from up front to get closer to Jay. He's pacing up and down the aisle looking for Lisa. He points the gun at every single aisle.

Cecily breaks cover and charges. Jay never sees her coming until he's knocked on his ass. He looks at her startled, but the half a second it took to do that is too long. She starts pounding his face with the flat of her fist. She feels his nose snap and hears him gurgle.

Cecily feels pain in her neck and her vision distorts. The echo of a gunshot is ringing in her head. She rolls to the side and grabs her neck. Blood spills from a wound that was caused by her own neglect. She didn't pay attention to what Jay was doing with the gun and now that one bullet has found its home.

Jay stands above her and kicks her hard in the stomach.

"You know," he says. "I was going to let you live. Take my daughter and fucking go. But no, you had to brainwash her."

He kicks her a few more times and points the gun to her head.

"Genesis two twenty-two," he says, kicking her in the chin. "The Lord God fashioned into a woman the rib which He had taken from the man and brought her to the man. You see how funny that is? You're not even a whole person. You're just a rib. You're just a fucking rib!"

He pulls the trigger, and nothing happens. He swings the gun downward and smashes Cecily's nose.

"Hey, Dad," says a voice behind him. He turns to see Lisa standing there with a giant blade. She swings it in an arch, and it slices through his throat like a string through a block of cheese. His eyes go wide, and he feels blood pouring like a waterfall from the wound. He shakes his head back and forth. He reaches his hands out to Lisa to beg for forgiveness.

The only thing he finds is Brittany's hands as they finish breaking the fingers Cecil didn't. When he falls back, she's on him, punching and stabbing with a set of keys.

Jay's last vision is the face of his daughter smiling.

Cecily crawls to Jay. She puts her hand on Brittany and makes her stop. She feels around in Jay's pocket for anything she can use. She finds a flip phone that got broken in half at some point in the night. She puts it in her mouth and chews it into pieces. She takes the wristwatch from the other pocket and does the same.

The hole in her neck seals and her mouth turns into a nest for metal and plastic worms.

"Protect her," she says to Brittany as she stands up.

Brittany nods and grabs Lisa's arm. They hide in the back of the church and wait to see what happens.

Cecily marches forward and collides with one of the fucking children. She stumbles over. She gets back to her feet and watches as these fucking troublemakers kill Lisa's first creation. She stands in the midst of flying teeth and bone fragments like they're nothing.

She sees the girl rolling under pews and meets her at the front of the church as Lisa's creation falls. She grabs the girl by the hair and moves toward the Baptismal tub...

CHAPTER
TWENTY-FOUR

Whoever said drowning was the most peaceful way to go was an asshole, in Billy's opinion. Of course, that could have been different if she weren't pinned to the bottom of a plastic tub by someone's foot. Drowning in the ocean, a peaceful lake, a creek, even a puddle would be better than this.

She thrashes and kicks. She digs her nails into Cecily's leg. She can taste the rusty penny flavor mixing into the stale water. Nothing works. She hears splashing and feels Cecily moving. She tries to take the opportunity to move, but the foot puts more pressure on her head.

Her lights start to dim. She feels her body starting to work against her. She tells herself magicians do this for way longer. She also knows she isn't a magician because she isn't quite that big of an asshole.

Finally, she inhales.

Ethan tries to get to his feet again. He did it once, charged the tub, and met another backhand. The same happened to Dylan. They both lay on opposite sides of the room in pain, unable to do anything.

Ethan uses the altar to stand up and watches Cecily step out of the tub.

He knows there's only one reason she would be stepping out.

His anger takes over, and he runs at her again. He meets Dylan at Cecily and they both start throwing punches at her. She takes each blow like it isn't even happening. Ethan swings as hard as he can and hits her on the tip of the nose. Her head doesn't even move. She's just absorbing punch after punch like they're giving her energy.

Molly appears and hits Cecily with a board she got from somewhere. For whatever reason, this pissed Cecily off. She was taking the punches and laughing like they were coming from ants. But the board, that sent her over some sort of edge.

"Do you want to drown too, you fucking traitor?" Cecily says. She grabs Molly around her throat and slams her on top of the fallen crucifix. "I think the world needs a new messiah. A new image on the cross. Molly, I choose you to die for the sins of women everywhere who have let men rule them like they are nothing more than cattle."

"While I agree with the sentiment," Molly says. "I'd rather not." She pulls a wire-gun and shoots it point blank into Cecily's left eye. When she pulls the trigger, the eyeball pops like a grape.

Cecily rips the wire from her dead eye. She grabs the board Molly hit her with and swats it at the charging Ethan and Dylan. The blow sends them flying back into the baptismal tub.

Cecily breaks the board. She gets a long sliver of wood and stabs it through Molly's left hand, pinning her to the cross.

Molly reaches out and jams her thumb into Cecily's dead eye. She feels wires moving around like maggots. She can feel gears connecting and turning over.

Cecily just smiles.

"Watched one movie too many, haven't we?" Cecily says, pulling Molly's arm from her face. She holds it down and picks up another chunk of wood. She holds it over her head, ready to stab the other hand.

"Hey, Cecily!" A voice says behind her. She turns and sees a soaking-wet Billy holding a shotgun in her face. She smiles because she knows this can't hurt her.

She notices the wires going into the barrel just in time to turn her face to anger before the trigger is pulled.

The bullet leaves pushing the needles out of the barrel with it. The electric current and holy water coating it like a weapon built for hunting demons. When it enters the front of Cecily's head, it goes to war with everything inside. The water finds all the evil and drowns it out. The wires sizzle and writhe like worms that have just had boiling hot water poured all over their bodies. Cecily's body tries to fight it, but between the force of the bullet hitting her brain, and the work of the wire-gun, she can do nothing but slump forward.

Molly sees all of it happen in a blur. When Cecily falls beside her, she can see Billy standing there. She's got needles from the wire-gun piercing her skin all over. The water is still steaming from the electrical charges.

"I knew it would be like a big electric bathtub," says Dylan. "I feel like Dr. Frankenstein now."

"Not just yet," says Billy. "Shocking my heart back into rhythm after drowning is a lot different from reanimating me from a cold, dead corpse."

Ethan squats by Molly and looks at the wound in her hand.

"Just rip it out," Molly says. "We're leaving now anyway, right? Please say yes."

Ethan gives her a small smile before grabbing the sliver of wood and ripping it out. He wraps the wound with a towel he found by the tub.

"She smells like burnt dog shit," Billy says, looking at Cecily.

They see the front door of the church swing open as Lisa and Brittany run out of it at full speed.

"How the fuck," Dylan says.

His question is answered when the baptismal tub explodes upwards, and tentacles emerge like a Kaiju-sized octopus leaving a tunnel. One of the tentacles wraps around Cecily and drags her into the tunnel below.

All is quiet and they wonder if it's finally over. Is that all the thing wanted? The person who was starting so much shit?

The chattering of teeth fills the air. It's so loud it sounds like it's coming through a sound system.

They all look at each other and start to run to the front of the church.

The building shakes, wood falling all around them. Molly is the first one out the door. Billy is behind her, followed by Ethan and then Dylan. When they're almost to the small room at the front of the church, they're cut off by the massive tail of a snake.

That's the best they can come up with in their head.

It looks like an overgrown spine, every bit fifty feet long. It slithers and glides as easily as a snake. The body connects to a massive amount of flesh that functions as a mouth with billions of teeth.

"I am the great Serpent's eyes and ears," says Cecily. Her body has been absorbed into the flesh. Her torso sticks out of the top of the giant cavern of teeth like this is where she has always belonged. "A fallen angel made into the image of the first fallen angel. Eve would be proud." Her hands caress the top of the thing.

It dives at the three still in the church but overshoots, clearly not quite comfortable in the open or with its new eyes.

They dodge and run to the front of the church. Billy looks down into the hole where the thing came from.

And sees it's a perfectly round concrete pipe. Beside the pipe stands the ghost she saw at college. He wears a robe made of locusts and the smile of a used car salesman. Billy flips him off as a thank you for being absolutely no help at all.

"Hey, dickheads!" she yells. "Let's skate."

Ethan grabs her board and his. Dylan gets his new gift from Marcus and the book bag with wire-guns. They each grab two each, leaving an odd one. Billy takes it and sticks it in her back pocket.

The fallen Angel sees what they're doing and charges. Billy is the first to go down the incline. Ethan and Dylan shake their heads and follow into the tunnel.

CHAPTER
TWENTY-FIVE

If Dylan's dad knew there was a completely lit underground tunnel that works as a full pipe, he kept that one to himself. And why wouldn't he? The fact that there are lights on raise so many questions. Questions no one has time for right now as they speed down a tunnel that goes up, down, left, right, up, down. Why make a tunnel this confusing and long?

All over the walls are religious symbols, some too old to take a guess at. Some just hastily drawn crosses. Some look like a painter took one hundred centuries to paint, others look like a toddler had a Sharpie and no supervision. They try to read them as they flash past. Some of the symbols are used as marking points to the trio to see how high up on the wall they should, or should not, go.

Billy is the fastest, as always. She powers through each corner and over each little upward slope. She feels like she's in a never-ending skatepark. She tries not to go up the walls too high, doesn't want to give that thing anytime to catch up. It's probably just moving straight whereas the others have to use the transitions for speed.

After what feels like a mile of endless transition, they enter a huge concrete globe. From the tunnel, a slight hill drops them into the inside of the concrete ball. Seeing the inside of where the angel has spent countless decades is surreal. Imagining being trapped in a concrete globe with one blueish light overhead for as long as history can recall.

They roll over the sides and through the flat to the far wall just in time to see the Cecily-thing emerge from the entrance. It lets out a shriek as it finds its way back to where it started.

Ethan carves toward her and shoots out one of his wires before pumping back over the entrance. He gains speed and comes back in on the other side of the thing. He can see Billy shooting both of her wires. Both connect in Cecily's head.

The creature lunges at Dylan. Its teeth clacking together on empty air. He carves under its teeth and shoots the wire. It wraps around one of the teeth, so he does the same with his second. The thing turns and swats its tail out.

Ethan shoots at the body of the thing but hits the tail as it swoops at him. He feels a blow hit him full-on. The force sends his body up higher into the wall and he crashes down onto the concrete on his feet. His left ankle turns to the side, and he hears the snapping of bones. He feels it in his teeth.

He sits up, groaning in pain. He feels the length of his leg down to the ankle. A bone is protruding through the skin on the outside and his foot is totally numb. He realizes he's fucked as soon as the Cecily thing puts its face right against his. It opens its mouth, showing all the teeth floating around like a galaxy of lacerations. It smells like someone who hasn't drunk water in a decade and has only eaten meat.

He watches Dylan and Billy carve on the wall behind him. They're going so fast they go over the entranceway to the place. He hears their wheels coming back down and heading toward him.

Cecily's head turns to watch Dylan and Billy as they carve high above Ethan and the teeth. They both shoot another wire and pull the triggers.

The thing's mouth has steam pouring out of it; it feels warm and rancid on Ethan's body. He rolls himself away from what's happening.

The thing stretches to its full height and breaks through the roof of the globe. Sunlight and dirt pour in. The wires are too much to take mixed with the introduction of the morning sun and it falls back to the floor. It writhes on the ground furiously before flying toward the entrance.

Dylan and Billy slow down and hop off their boards by Ethan.

"That's fucking gross!" says Dylan, looking at the ankle.

"It's not that bad," says Ethan sarcastically.

"I think you're probably going to get left down here forever. How are we going to get him out?"

"We'll worry about that later," says Billy. "But right now, we've really got to finish that thing off. It headed back up the tunnel so it may be hiding. I have an idea."

They set Ethan on his skateboard and manage to push him all the way back to the entrance of the baptismal tub.

The church is ominously quiet. All the bodies are gone from the chapel. There is no sign of the things exit anywhere. Did it somehow teleport or vanish into thin air?

Dylan hears wood groan above him. He taps Ethan and Billy on the shoulders and points up. Above them is a thing made of bone and machinery. The size of a bear, it rests on the rafters. Its skin is held together by wires like stitches. The wires move like snakes going in and out of tunnels. Its flesh has punctures all over from the teeth below breaking free. It's taken everybody in this place and molded the flesh together to create some humanoid monstrosity of flesh, bone, teeth, and electronics. Swings down by its back feet and hangs upside down like a bat. Its arms stretch out for the three. The hands end in broken femur bones that it uses as talons. Sitting on the shoulders is the head of Cecily. What used to be Cecily. She's vaguely recognizable, as even her mouth has been stretched to the limits to hold all the new teeth.

From behind its back, giant wings made of bone and stretched flesh open. It drops away from the rafter and soars over their heads. It hits the wall behind them with its feet and kicks off toward them again. It hits Dylan full force with its tooth-covered body and lifts him in the air.

Dylan puts his hands on the body and tries to free himself. The teeth pierce through his skin just like they did his clothes. He's stuck dangling as the thing flies to the ceiling.

It grabs him with its arms and holds him out over the rafters. It either plans to drop him or spike him like a football. He sees a purple glow behind its eyes. Maybe the power source? He doesn't finish the thought as the thing bites into his forearm. It swings him back and forth like a cat's toy before sending him flying into a wall.

"The head!" he yells. He feels his chest hurt as the words escape. "Aim for the eyes or something. Fucking thing has a purple glow back there.

The thing swoops down toward Billy. She swings her board at it and connects with the head. It crashes into her, and both sail back into the opening of the tunnel. They teeter on the lip as the thing snaps at Billy's face. She jerks her head backwards twice, using the incline as a way to avoid the rows of teeth.

Ethan stands to his feet. His broken ankle screams out through his nerves in pain. He collapses from the shock of how bright and brilliant the pain is. He gets his good leg under him and says fuck it. He pushes through the pain and makes it to a rifle laying haphazardly on the stage. He grimaces through the pain of bone grinding on bone and one grinding into the ground as he walks toward Billy and the Cecily-bat. He falls on the thing's back and points the gun toward its head.

Bones crack, wires shift, the thing's head spins around to face him on a neck that is stretching like elastic.

"Fuck no," he says as he points the rifle and pulls the trigger. The bullet hits the head in the right eye. Pieces of skull explode outward. The purple light Dylan mentioned is exposed to the air.

Billy acts fast and pulls the last wire-gun from her waist and shoots it into the light. When it pierces the thing, the light begins to glow before quickly dimming.

The Cecily-bat takes a few backward steps before toppling over off the stage and in front of the altar. It lands with its destroyed head beside the head of Jesus on the cross. Blood begins to pour from the opening as the body deflates, just like the others. The wings lift up and try to flap to safety one time before splashing down in the blood and remaining lifeless.

"Dylan!" yells Ethan. "Are you alive?"

"No," says Dylan. "It bit the fuck out of my arm. It looks like a shark bite. And I think I have some broken ribs."

"Join the club," says Billy, sitting up and grabbing her chest in pain.

Dylan crawls across the floor to the altar to meet Billy and Ethan. They all look at each other and start laughing the laugh of three people who just went through a fever dream of violence.

"What the fuck was all of that?" Billy says.

"Ethan," says Dylan. "If you wanted us to spend more time with you, just tell us. Don't go to all this trouble. It wasn't fun at all."

The front door swings open and Molly is standing in the morning light with two men dressed head to toe in swat gear.

"What the fuck," says Billy. "I think your girlfriend called the SWAT team."

"She's not my girlfriend," Ethan says. There's a hint of disappointment in his voice. Or it could be the pain radiating through his body. Either way, it doesn't matter because Molly is hugging him so tightly that the pain is doubled and he's not so sure she isn't going to be his girlfriend in time.

"Who are the meatheads?" Dylan asks.

"Oh, yeah," Molly says. "Craziest shit. They're going to need to talk to you."

CHAPTER TWENTY-SIX

It's always black SUVs that show up to things like this. The government-issued coverup vehicle. If you've been a part of something, and you see these; you know you're going to be asked to shut up about whatever it was.

Billy rolls her eyes when she sees the door open. A man dressed in a black tuxedo steps out and extends his hand for a shake. She watches as Ethan shakes it; he's not going to cause any trouble. Dylan shakes it; too annoyed to care and stuck doing whatever Ethan does because he's his second leg right now. When it's her turn, she looks at the hand. She thinks about biting it. She thinks about pulling a Cecily and breaking all the guy's fingers. Instead, she shakes her head no and gets in the SUV.

Instantly, she regrets it. It's not set up like a regular car. The only real seats are the front two. A window separates them from the driver. The seats in the back run parallel along the walls of the vehicle so that all parties involved can see one another clearly. Molly, Ethan, Dylan, and Billy all sit on one side like prisoners locked together by a chain. Three men sit across from them. The man who held the door open gets in and squeezes between two of the others.

The windows are blacked out. No one can see in, no one can see out. They're stuck for as long as whatever this is takes. They didn't even show them any weapons, so how do they know these people could have forced them? Billy regrets not saying no at first. When she saw Molly's hand was bandaged up, she assumed they were taking care of them medically. Considering Ethan's ankle, that's the most important thing.

One of the men instantly starts rubbing a cream on the wound and messing with some stuff in a medical bag. He pops the ankle out and sets it back in place before Ethan has a chance to debate the matter. He just looks at it and squints his eyes.

"It doesn't hurt at all," Ethan says.

"It's a little numbing trick we know," says the mystery man. "My name is Denver. That's Idaho, Cali, and our man fixing that ankle is New Ham."

"How come they're all states, but you're a city?" Billy asks.

"Good question. Maybe because I just have a real soft spot for John Denver."

Billy doesn't believe the fake charm. Two motionless guys sitting on either side of him says one thing to her: threatening. She leans back in the chair and watches New Ham wrap Ethan's ankle with a cast. She's not going to be the one to do the talking first. No way.

"Where did my car go?" asks Billy.

"Oh," says Molly. "I tried to stop them, but my hand was a mess. The older one flipped me off and took off. I was eating apples in the RV when these guys showed up. Can you believe all they had in that RV to eat was apples?"

"So," says Dylan. "What's all this about then?"

"Ah," says Denver. "You found something you shouldn't have. As I'm sure you've gathered, we're members of The Right Hand of Adam, the same organization that helped Pastor Jay help you all."

"If by help you mean cause a bigger mess that almost got all of us killed, then yes. Yes, he absolutely did do that. Fucking moron."

"He wasn't a member. The point is, we need you all to keep quiet about what happened here tonight. We're willing to compensate you. We're willing to give you work. We just can't let this out of the bag. It goes against God's will."

"Give me a million-" says Dylan before he's cut off by Molly.

"You know, I got kidnapped from work. I was minding my own business, and I got stuck in an RV with those crazy assholes and forced here. I had no horse in the race. Was it God's will to make me suffer for no conceivable reason? And I don't want to hear that whole 'lord works in mysterious ways' bullshit. You can shove that stuff up your ass. Sure seems like if God didn't want that to happen, he could have floated his fat ass down here and helped out a little. What? Did he have something better to do? It sure as shit isn't solving any of the problems in the world. Let me guess, some old white guy needed his favorite fucking sports team to win a game, so God was a little busy answering those prayers? We don't want compensation, you fucker. Let me out of this car."

Molly stands up to leave, car still in motion. She looks back at Ethan, sighs, and sits back down.

"Is this how all of you feel?"

They all nod.

"My fucking chest hurts, dude," says Billy. "How long did you have this SWAT team outside? We could have used some help. Or was that not God's will?"

"What can I do to make this problem go away for all of us?"

They all look at each other.

Finally, Billy speaks up.

SUMMER
2024

EPILOGUE

The world never stopped rotating on its axis. The oceans never dried up. Things are getting that bad, sure. Thanks to humans taking advantage of Mother Nature, but not overnight like it should have. A steady decline is one thing. They're doing that to themselves, but the overnight flash bang signifying the end was where it was at. Humanity was making slow work, destroying themselves. Sure, the wars, disease, fights, famines, and every other manner of destroying each other was working; it just wasn't working fast enough. Cecily would have had this whole damn place eradicated years ago; long before climate change could do it.

Everything has grown in twenty years. It's easier now to find people who you can relate to on social media. Food from anywhere can be delivered right to your door. You can find out any little bit of information at the click of a button and the swoop of your hand. It's exactly what Lisa needed. Most importantly to Lisa, it's easier to find followers.

When MySpace started taking off, Lisa knew there were opportunities. She knew she could get some followers. She had her father's natural charisma, so she could bring people over to her side in a hurry. It started slowly. No one believed her. No one wants to believe the crazy girl on the internet who says she knows the location of a fallen Angel. But before long, people started noticing that Lisa was the kind of person you wanted to be around. She was attractive, funny, smart, and downright convincing when it came to her cause. But these things didn't win everyone over. There were still some who doubted every word she said. Some who selfishly only thought of themselves.

What's in it for me, huh?

The other usual question. She would promise riches, power, sex, anything! Often times these people's greed could be appealed to. She would show them what her organization did for the most passionate and loyal of followers, and they would jump in headfirst.

She also wrote those people down in her book of names in the section labeled, "dying as soon as this is finished." You don't ask for proof to do something, if you believe; if you don't, then convincing you of greed proved one thing. You could be bought out.

She used people, she manipulated people, she did things that would have made Cecily proud. But she refused to let people use her. If you want all The Daughters of Eve have to offer, you better follow in line and not demand a reward.

When Brittany took her out of the church and forced her into that small four-door car, she thought life was over. She thought she would be on the run for a week or two and then get caught.

No one ever caught them.

It was like no one was even looking.

They killed men of God all over the country. They met new follow-ers, most of which had to be left at home for the bigger plan. Just Lisa and Brittany. That was the way she wanted it, and Brittany was fine with that, too. Two women doing exactly what their mentor showed them to do on the road to their destinies.

There were days when Brittany struggled. Some days it was every-thing the poor woman could do to not kill herself. Those days, noth-ing got done and Lisa would just stare at the screen of whatever phone she had stolen.

Brittany began to move on over time. She knew Cecily had sacri-ficed herself for the good of both Lisa and her. She couldn't let her lover and mentor's sacrifice go for nothing. She began working on controlling her anger. She had somehow become colder and more calculated than even Cecily. She was Lisa's wrath, sent down from a skyscraper in NYC to punish anyone who dared to try to make a fool out of anyone in Cecily Incorporated.

They made their money selling electronic gadgets to stores all over the world. Machines that shouldn't work as good as they did, yet they defied logic and worked. The companies would pay Lisa's company to create a blueprint for a device that would make their work easier.

Lisa loved hearing about the amount of money in payroll. One of her devices had saved a company. She would laugh and joke with Brittany about the people they made miserable every night.

Two decades flew by in a hurry. In Lisa's mind, it was just last week that she showed up at Heath's house and gutted him like a fish. She still wishes she could have been there to see his family's reaction to finding their son cut open and spread out on the dining room table like a Thanksgiving feast.

Too busy to stick around. She did keep an eye on the news to see what people said about everything. That was a crock, for the most part as all the deaths at the church were explained away as a gas leak. Same bullshit explanation for every single cover-up ever.

She keeps tabs on Ethan, Billy, and Dylan. She watched them closely. Ethan and Molly have two kids. Billy and her partner own a record shop in town. Dylan and Maria have one son.

All three of them own a skatepark as a partnership. The skatepark features a snake run that ends in a concrete globe, and... an indoor pool. She would often become infuriated that these three had made a joke out of Cecily's resting place.

She's followed breadcrumbs and conspiracy theories online enough to know that Adam's stooges paid people off and gave them the church. The blogs and Twitter accounts all know about it. There are at least seventy YouTube videos about it. It's a cover-up bigger than Roswell.

"Hey, girl," says Brittany. It breaks Lisa out of her trance. "Colton wants to know when we should do this?"

"Tell him that today is the day," says Lisa.

She goes to her computer and waves her hand above the keyboard. Wires move like tentacles and attach to the side of her head. Her phone is picked up and connected to the mainframe of her own brain, too.

She sends tweets; she reposts theories; she spreads misinformation. With her new setup, she can do all of these things in seconds. The internet has become her Beehive, and she is the queen giving out orders and watching it all come together.

She's made over a thousand Twitter accounts. All linked together to post the same thing at the same time. She's built a list of loyal followers and servants who believe she is right; people who believe that Lisa Barnett will control everything in the world. No one will be able to exist without confirming it with Lisa first.

"Tell me when you're ready," says Brittany.

Lisa nods.

The plan is simple. Send a spell as a tweet. All the phones, computers, watches that the tweet is seen on will turn into her little creations. They mimic those of Cecily but are much more advanced. With the advancement of technology came the advancement of her death machines. She can make a simple cell phone into a time bomb now. She can make a set of wireless headphones into flying death machines.

When she sends out this spell, she will become one with all the devices that see it. She will control all the technology. She will become the queen bee in the world's busiest hive.

"I'm ready..." she says to Brittany. Brittany nods and turns on her device.

First, she sends a command to Colton's computer in California. The computer turns into a creature that resembles an octopus and wraps its wire limbs around Colton. She can feel it pulling him closer before it explodes and takes the creator and all the info of the project with it.

She goes to Twitter.

She enters the text.
"Respira vitam, machina Satanae."
Send tweet.

ACKNOWLEDGEMENTS

Thank you to my wife, Breanna. I couldn't do this without you always being there for me and being down for pizza and Return of the Killer Tomatoes weekly.

Thank you to Mercedes Varnado for inspiring me to be the person I've always wanted to be.

Thank you to Joey at Mad Axe for taking this book on and showing it love.

Thank you to every single person in the horror community who supports me with friendship and appreciation of my work. You don't know how much just tolerating my dumb ass means to me. Write your name here so it's personal:

____

Thankee in the biggest way to you, the reader. If you're reading this that means you took a chance on my work and enjoyed it enough to finish it. I appreciate that more than you know. You deserve to have your name in this book. Please write your name below:

____